THE ARCHER HOUSE

THE ARCHER INN SERIES BOOK ONE

KIMBERLY THOMAS

The Archer House
The Archer Inn Series
Book One
By
Kimberly Thomas

CHAPTER ONE

"Watch out, coming through!" A deep, booming voice nearly gave Holly a heart attack. She had just enough time to jump back to avoid getting ran over by the two large men carrying a wooden dresser down the hallway. Their muscles bulged beneath the tight t-shirts, and Holly thanked God she had the sense to hire people to do the heavy lifting for her. There was no way she would have ever been able to move that dresser on her own.

It wasn't just the heavy furniture the crew was hauling away, though. All around her were men and a few women packing boxes and carrying them out of the house. Her heart ached each time a box was carried through the large double doors at the front of the house. Over twenty years, she had lived in this house. And now it was all coming to a close. The final chapter in this part of her life was coming to an official close and really tugged at her heart strings.

Holly steadied herself against the banister, looking down at the workers as they busied themselves packing and moving her things.

Not everything was going, of course. Will's stuff would remain behind. But even with that, the place already looked empty. Mementos from their various trips together over the years were already packed into boxes and loaded onto the moving truck. Photos that had hung on the walls for years were gone, leaving unfaded squares of paint in their places.

It should have given her relief, severing off this part of her life like a rotting limb on a tree. But instead, it just made her heart break more and more with each passing moment. This wasn't just a single branch of her life she was trimming away; it was more like chopping down the entire tree right at the base.

Holly squeezed her eyes shut. In and out, she told herself silently, focusing on her breathing and trying to push everything else out of her mind. But no matter how many times she repeated the words to herself, she couldn't quite block out the hustle and bustle going on all around her.

She needed some space, she decided. It was too painful to stand around the house and watch her life be boxed up and carted away by strangers.

Without saying a word to anyone, she made her way downstairs and through the expansive home. It had never seemed this big before, but whether she had just never noticed or if the lack of belongings made it seem even larger than it was, Holly couldn't help but feel like the place was preparing to swallow her whole.

Her car was parked right out front, thankfully not blocked in by the moving trucks. Before she knew it, she was heading down the highway away from the place she had called home for so long. It wasn't until she pulled into her parking spot at the office that she realized where she had headed.

She'd driven there on autopilot in a haze, not even stopping to think. She had just wanted to get away from the house and the chaos and memories that had threatened to overwhelm her. Not that the office would be much better, she thought as she watched a muscular man step out of the front door carrying a large box.

Wanting to be efficient, and also to just rip the band-aid off right away, she had scheduled the movers to not only pack up and haul away the stuff at the house but to also do the same at her office. Well, her former office now. Just like the house, running the business she had devoted most of her adult life to would be left to her now ex-husband, Will.

With a sigh, she killed the car's engine. Sitting in the vehicle staring at the building wasn't going to make things any easier. Nor was turning around and going back to the house. And, if she was being honest with herself, she wasn't sure where else she could go. Those two places had been her life for so long that she had pretty much forgotten how to live without them.

Heck, there were days and weeks when she had spent more time at the office than at the house, earning herself many dirty looks from the other moms whenever she showed up at the school or to retrieve the kids from playdates. To them, being a mom was their sole identity. She'd loved her kids to the moon and back, but she'd never understood dedicating her every waking moment to them like some mothers did. She had juggled motherhood and her career flawlessly while never neglecting her children.

And this made it easier when the kids eventually grew up and started their own lives. Of course, she had missed them, but it hadn't completely broken her when they had flown the coop like it had for the mothers of some of their friends. She loved her kids more than life itself and her kids knew that. She had a very special bond with them that no one could break. Not even her husband.

Though now, she understood how those women had felt. As she stared up at her office window, knowing the career she had spent years building and nurturing was finally over, she fully understood the pain those mothers had experienced. Her kids may not have made up the bulk of her identity, but her job as a top real estate agent in Miami certainly had.

She had busted her butt to be taken seriously as a real estate agent. And she'd been darn good at it, no matter what anyone else said. But of course, her greedy husband had to go and mess all of that up. No, she corrected, closing her eyes and taking another deep breath—ex-husband, not husband.

The man didn't deserve the title of husband anymore. It was hard to believe she had ever fallen in love with that man. Here she had thought they'd be together for the rest of their lives. As it turned out, he hadn't had the same notions. It had been over a year since the divorce had been finalized, and yet it was still hard to realize everything really was over with.

At least she'd had the forethought to store away some money separate from everything else. So while he was left broke and practically penniless, Holly at least still had some money to support herself and wouldn't be homeless once everything was said and done.

It was a small comfort, but it was better than nothing.

With another sigh, Holly popped the door of the Jaguar open and slid out, automatically straightening the wrinkles in her clothes out of habit. Not that it really mattered how she dressed anymore. She could show up wearing designer clothes that cost more than some people made in a year and it wouldn't improve her reputation even a smidge.

Will's illicit real estate dealings had seen to that.

Now it was a disgrace for her just to show her face in the grocery stores these days. Certainly, no one was interested in hiring her anymore, which was the main reason she was having her office packed up and carted away. That and she couldn't stand to share a space with Will anymore. It had been hard enough after the divorce. Now, it just wasn't going to happen.

The further away from him she could get the better. At least, that was what she was hoping for.

When she finally made her way into the office, she was surprised just how bustling it was. It wasn't full of customers, of course, but most of the employees were still hovering around. Groups of two or three huddled together, talking in harsh whispers as they watched the spectacle around them.

All eyes turned to her when she stepped through the door, and Holly could feel their judgmental gazes burning through her. Not only had Will's schemes ruined her reputation around town and within the industry, but even her own employees seemed to have lost respect for her.

She caught some of their whispers as she walked by, but she pretended not to hear any of them. She didn't want to show just how much their snippy comments actually hurt.

"How could she not have known?" one of the secretaries whispered to another one. Both had their eyes boring into Holly as she passed by them, but Holly refused to return their gaze. There was a time when she would have quashed that kind of talk in an instant.

Those days were in the past, though, much like everything else about her former life.

"It's not her fault her husband was a snake," the other secretary whispered back, and Holly had to force down a smile. At least everyone didn't think she was just as guilty as he was. That small comfort didn't last long, though before the woman continued. "All she ever cared about was work. Maybe if she'd been a better wife, he wouldn't have strayed off God's path."

Holly let out a sigh and quickly navigated the halls to her office. It was just as barren as her house had been, with nothing more than the furniture remaining. Everything personal had already been boxed up and carted away. It looked very much like it had the first day she had moved in all those years ago.

She walked over and stood behind her desk, surveying the openness in front of her. She could still remember that day clearly. She had been so young back then, having just gotten her realty license. She was ready to take the world by storm, with her husband right by her side. The brokerage firm had been his father's originally, and the two of them had been able to take it over and hit the ground running.

Back then, they had been untouchable. They'd thought they were untouchable and mingle with the crème of the crop and be rich forever. Holly had been head over heels in love with Will, awed by his skill in realty and his drive to always push things to the next level. But it got to the point that neither of them had ever been content with what they had, more so Will than Holly. He'd always wanted more regardless of the price they had to pay and of course Holly always followed suit blinded by love.

Maybe the gossip in the hall had been right, Holly thought to herself bitterly. If she hadn't been so caught up in taking the world by storm, she might've noticed the writing on the walls sooner. Maybe if she had spent more time with her family, she wouldn't have missed all the obvious clues that something wasn't right.

It was too late for any of that now, though. Everything was said and done with. Will's illicit dealings had cost the both of them their brokerage and realty licenses, and Holly doubted she would ever be able to get hers back even though she had nothing to do with any of it. Maybe if she packed everything up and moved to Alaska or something, she might be able to start fresh. She honestly doubted it, though.

But she was only forty-six with still so much life in her. But the idea of packing up and starting from scratch somewhere brand new just wasn't that appealing. And she had spent her entire life living in sunny Florida. Freezing her butt off in Alaska was not a pleasant prospect at all.

She had to figure out something, though. She couldn't just sit around here and do nothing. Sure, she had enough money put away that she didn't *need* to work, but not working just wasn't an option for her. She was liable to go crazy if she didn't have something to occupy her time. She had to keep busy and work at something that she could look back at and be proud of. She enjoyed working hard and she had instilled that work ethic in each of her children.

She just had to figure out how she could accomplish that now that realty wasn't in her future anymore. Going back to school at her age didn't seem all that interesting, though it wasn't completely out of the question. But if she did that, what would she study? What other field could she apply her skills and drive toward?

Law school was tempting, but by the time she finished, she

would be past her prime and she wasn't sure she wanted to deal with the stress and long hours it would take to establish herself in that field. Plus, there was a good chance all of this would follow her and ruin any chances she had of making a name for herself as a lawyer.

A knock on the door frame leading into her office jarred her out of her thoughts. She blinked a few times before reality came back, then she looked over to see Sandra, the woman who ran the office's mailroom, standing there. She smiled at Holly, a sad one, but at least she didn't have the same look of contempt in her eyes the others tended to have.

"Just had an envelope dropped off for you," Sandra said, quickly crossing the length of the room to hand Holly the manila envelope. There was no stamp or return address so clearly, it hadn't been sent through the mail.

But Holly knew that scrawl on the front of the envelope and just staring at it made a lump form in the back of her throat.

"T—thank you," Holly managed to stammer out. She forced a smile onto her face and tried not to show just how nervous she was right then. If Sandra was the only person left in the office that didn't hate her, then Holly didn't want to give her any reason to change that opinion.

Sandra smiled back and then slipped out of the office without another word, leaving Holly alone in the quiet, empty room once more.

Her hands shook as she opened the envelope, pulling out the sheets of paper stuffed inside. Just as expected, the paper on the top was a letter from her lawyer, the law firm's heading taking up the top few inches of the paper. Holly scanned the letter faster than she thought possible, her heart pounding the entire time, threatening to break through her rib cage.

The more she read, the closer she felt to a heart attack. She had hoped the letter might put some of her fears at ease. But instead, it did the exact opposite. It only served to confirm her worst nightmares.

Will's antics had already cost the both of them their brokerage and real estate licenses. But now, not only was he under criminal investigation, but so was she. The evidence compiled against her ex-husband was daunting, and even though she'd had no knowledge of any of it, she was implicated in a lot just by being associated with him.

Both of them were looking at jail time if her lawyer couldn't pull off some kind of miracle.

Holly dropped the papers onto her desk and just stared at them for a long while, trying to comprehend everything she had just read —her mind in a whirl.

As if she didn't already have enough on her plate! Now she had one more headache to deal with on top of everything else. She placed one hand over her mouth as a gasp escaped and then she felt a tear roll down her cheek.

Her tough outer shell threatened to shatter and she didn't know how much more of this she could take.

CHAPTER TWO

HOLLY'S HEART RATE CONTINUED TO SKYROCKET. BUT NOW, IT wasn't just anxiety fueling her. Instead, rage slowly eclipsed the anxiousness. Holly wiped her cheek, scooped the papers back up off the desk and then stormed out of her office, hands balled into fists. This time, when she crossed through the open areas, there were no snarky comments or pitying looks.

Everyone got out of her way. Movers and co-workers alike scrambled to get out of her path, not wanting Holly to take her anger out on them. Those she had worked with had seen her temper more than once, and none of them were ever eager to be on the receiving side of it. And while none of them were her target right then, Holly wasn't sure she would be able to contain herself if one of them opened their mouth and said something stupid this time.

But none of them did and moments later, Holly was sitting in the driver's seat of her Jag once again. She tossed the paperwork onto the passenger seat and reached out to take hold of the steering wheel. Her fingers wrapped tightly around the dark leather, squeezing like she was trying to break it off the dash.

Breathe in, breathe out, she told herself, closing her eyes and trying to force her anger back into its cage. There was a time and a place to let it all out, but driving down the freeway wasn't one of them. Before she went anywhere, she needed to get control of herself again. If not, she was liable to do something stupid or dangerous.

And while she wanted to throttle her ex-husband right then and there, she would have to wait until she was face to face with him. Driving angry was just going to make things worse, not better. And she knew perfectly well that anger would still be there, waiting, once she was in front of Will again.

It took a few moments, but eventually, she was calm enough to fish the keys out of her pocket and start the Jag. It roared to life, and Holly quickly made her way out of the parking lot and back toward the highway. She was careful to drive safely, but she wasn't wasting any time either.

The sooner she arrived at her ex's place, the sooner she could rip him a new one. And boy, did she plan on leaving a mark!

She had made sure to have a nest egg put aside for not only herself but for their kids, should they ever fall on hard times. She could handle having to move out of their six-thousand square foot home and quit the job she'd had as far back as she could remember. It hurt, it was tough, but it was doable and she would survive.

Going to prison because Will was a damn idiot? That was definitely not an option. She would sooner move to Alaska and live in an Igloo than let Will's stupidity drag her to jail. No, he was going to fix this problem, one way or another.

When Holly pulled the Jag into the driveway leading up to the large house, a pang of pain hit her heart. This was a house she was familiar with. It belonged to Will's mother. When everything had exploded, it was the only place he could go.

But, before then, Holly had been there countless times. She had brought the kids there often to visit with their grandmother. They'd had birthday and holiday parties there. She had even stayed there and helped care for her mother-in-law after she'd had her knee replaced. The woman had insisted she could manage just fine, but Holly had known better and insisted on helping out until she could walk again. It had been a couple of weeks of working from a guest room she had converted into an office, but Holly had always liked the older woman.

Even now, it was hard to think anything negative about her. Just because her son had turned out to be a complete idiot didn't mean Holly had to hate her mother-in-law too.

When she stepped out of the Jag, she kept her eyes laser-focused on the front door, refusing to let her gaze wander. Her anger still bubbled just below the surface, and she wasn't about to let a burst of nostalgia get in the way. Will had this outburst coming, and nothing was going to stop her from giving him the chewing out he so very much deserved.

Well, if she was being honest with herself, he deserved that and so much more.

Knocking on the front door, Holly listened to the thundering echoes through the house. Her mother-in-law had resisted getting a doorbell for some reason Holly had never understood. With a house that large, it just seemed silly not to have a doorbell. Case in point, Holly knocked a total of four times without getting an answer.

She knew Will was home. There was nowhere else for him to be if he wasn't at the office. With a sigh, Holly reached down and tried the doorknob, pleasantly surprised to find it unlocked. It didn't squeak even slightly as she opened the door, first listening for any source of noise to determine where her rat of an ex might have been hiding out.

When she didn't hear anything, she called out for him. "Will? It's Holly. Where are you? We need to talk!" Somehow, she managed to keep the bulk of her anger out of her voice. But Will was bound to know if Holly was there, it wasn't going to be a good conversation.

They'd long ago left behind courteous conversations. These days, they avoided talking to each other unless absolutely necessary. And even in those instances, things usually devolved into shouting matches fairly quickly.

Will didn't respond, of course, and Holly let out a sigh, closing the front door behind her. Hands-on hips, she surveyed the house and its surroundings. As far as she could tell, it was completely empty, but she knew that wasn't the truth. Will was in there, somewhere. She just had to find him.

Like a bloodhound on a mission, Holly made her way through the house, searching for her prey. It didn't take long to find Will in the sunroom at the back of the house, lounging on a couch with his feet up on the coffee table as he watched TV. For a moment, she just stood there and stared at him. This wasn't the man she had married. The man she had fallen in love with never would have sat around dressed like a slob, just flipping through channels aimlessly.

He had always been just like her, unable to sit around and do nothing for very long. But while she had kept herself busy during this fiasco, he'd apparently given up. When he picked up a glass from the table beside him, Holly snorted. It didn't take a genius to realize he was drinking whiskey before it was even lunchtime.

The pity she felt for him only lasted for a few moments before the anger welled up once again and overpowered everything else. She stalked into the room, and then tossed the stack of paperwork onto the table. "Just when I thought you couldn't mess up my life any more than you already have, I find out there's a chance we might go to jail because you owe the IRS more money than God!"

Will blinked up at her in surprise. Had he really not heard Holly pounding on the front door and calling his name? Then again, if he was already drinking this early, maybe that wasn't out of the realm of possibility. "Good to see you, too," Will replied, his voice dripping with sarcasm. He glanced at the pile of papers in front of him, and then shrugged them off.

That just enraged Holly even more. He may have given up and accepted his fate, but she sure as heck hadn't! He had dug this grave, and now it was up to him to fill it back in, either with dirt or his own body. He wasn't going to drag her down with him, not if she could help it.

"You need to get with the IRS and figure this out before both of us land in jail," Holly demanded. Hands-on hips, she stood just a few feet away from him, glaring. For a brief moment, she had a flashback to when their son was a kid and had done something to land himself in hot water. But this time, it wasn't her ten-year-old son she was scolding. It was her forty-nine-year-old ex-husband who should've been well beyond needing a talking to.

"I'll handle it," Will answered with another shrug of his shoulders. His words were slurred slightly, confirming this glass of whiskey wasn't his first one this morning.

Holly gritted her teeth together. She had the urge to snatch the glass out of his hand and toss it across the room. If they had still been married, she would have probably done just that. Maybe it would've snapped him out of this funk he was in and back to reality.

But they weren't married anymore Holly reminded herself. If he wanted to be an alcoholic slob, then that was his problem, not hers. As long as he fixed the crap with the IRS or at the very least told them she had nothing to do with it, she didn't much care what happened to him.

That thought was almost as shocking as the letter she had just gotten. It was hard to believe how little she actually cared about this man anymore. It almost made her laugh to realize how different things were between the two of them. Any semblance of love she had once felt for him had gone out the window a long time ago.

And she really shouldn't have been surprised. After all, this wasn't the man she had loved for over two decades. This was someone else, someone she didn't even recognize anymore. She was just glad the kids were all grown now and hadn't had to go through this when they were younger.

"Damn it, Will. I've already lost everything because of your damn scheming behind my back! I'm not going to jail because you're an idiot and a snake!" Holly's anger continued to mount as she shouted at her ex. Her hands balled into fists, her nails biting into the soft flesh of her palms. "So stop sitting there wallowing in your own self-pity and fix this somehow! Because, by God, I will not take the fall for you!"

"Like you've ever taken a fall for me!" Will snapped back at her. He slammed his glass down on the side table, causing some of the amber liquid to slosh out. There was fire in his eyes now; bringing him just a step closer toward the man she had once known.

"And what is that supposed to mean?"

Will snorted and rolled his eyes. His lips were pursed tight as he shook his head. "You know damn well what I mean! You've never loved me, not ever. All you ever cared about was your career and the kids. You didn't give a crap what I did, and you only care now because it's ruined your precious career."

"Oh please," Holly spat at him, rolling her own eyes. "If I hadn't loved you, I would have never married you. I didn't need a husband to be a successful real estate agent, thank you. Yes, I loved my job. Yes, I love my kids more than life, but don't you dare sit there and act like I didn't love you just as much!"

She opened her mouth to yell at him some more but was cut off by the sound of her phone ringing. She clamped her mouth shut again and settled for silently glaring at him as she fished the phone out of her pocket. The damned thing seemed to be stuck in there, and she said a mental curse toward whoever designed women's pants to have such small, tight pockets. Even getting custom tailored pantsuits hadn't been much help in mitigating that, but she hated carrying a purse or handbag.

Holly didn't even glance at the name on the screen before accepting the call. "Hello?" she said her voice a bit curter than she had wanted, but it was hard to keep her annoyance completely under wraps. She still had quite a bit to say to her ex, and the phone call was only delaying that.

"Holly, is that you?" the aging voice on the other end of the line asked. Hearing that voice, Holly's heart ached and she immediately regretted the snappy way she had answered the phone.

"Yes, it's me. What's wrong, Uncle Roger?" Holly could hear in just those words that this wasn't going to be a pleasant social call. And why would it be? She hadn't talked to the man in years. Technically he wasn't her uncle. He was her mother's cousin, but she had always grown up calling him Uncle and it seemed strange to call him anything else.

The man let out a sigh audible on the other end of the phone line. He had to be in his late sixties by now, and as far as Holly knew, he was still the accountant for the family Inn down in the Florida Keys. He had managed the business's finances for as long as Holly could remember. Another sigh came through the line before Roger spoke again. "It's your mother, Holly. Something's wrong."

Her heart had been pounding earlier, but now it didn't seem to be beating at all. The last time she had gotten a call like this, it had been two years ago when she had lost her father to a heart attack. She said a quick, silent prayer that her mother hadn't suffered a similar fate. "Is... is she...?" Holly's voice cracked. She couldn't even get the words out to finish her sentence.

"She's fine," Roger clarified, and Holly nearly collapsed with relief. With everything else going on, she couldn't stand the thought of losing her mother too. That would've just been too much for her to handle. "But something's wrong with her and the Archer Inn. You need to come back."

Holly's heart had restarted itself, and now it was slowly picking up the pace again. Go back? To the Florida Keys? To the Archer House? She hadn't been back there since her father had died two years ago. And even before then, she had seldom visited. Once she had left the Keys, she hadn't really looked back.

But if her mother needed her, then what was stopping her? She glanced over at Will, who still sat on the couch, glaring at her. At least he'd had the common sense not to interrupt her call, she thought bitterly. But with everything here in Miami in shambles, what was keeping her there? By tomorrow morning, everything she still owned would be moved out of the house and the office. She didn't have any other work lined up.

Sure, she still had the kids nearby, but they weren't exactly kids anymore. They were both grown with families of their own now. While she had no doubt they would both welcome the chance to spend some extra time with their mother, they didn't need her there. They would be just fine if she drove down to the Keys to find out what was going on with her mother and the family Inn.

So why was she so anxious about that prospect?

She took a deep breath and held it for a long moment, closing her eyes. When she let out the breath, some of her anxiety went along with it, but she knew it wouldn't go away forever. Not that it really mattered. No matter how anxious she was about returning to her childhood home or stressed out over Will and his shenanigans, she knew what her answer was.

"Okay, Roger. I'll be there," Holly told Roger. If her mother needed her, then there was no other answer to give him.

They spoke for a moment longer, and then Holly stuffed the phone back into her pocket. Her anger toward Will had lessened, replaced with worry for her mother, and all she had the energy for was to glare at Will. "Don't think this is over for a minute," she warned him. "Straighten things out with the IRS. I don't care how you do it; just do it!"

She didn't give him a chance to respond. She turned on her heel and stalked out of the sunroom without another word.

CHAPTER THREE

SUNLIGHT PEERED THROUGH THE WINDOW, AND HOLLY groaned. She rolled over in bed and pulled the covers up over her eyes in an attempt to block it out. But no matter how hard she tried, she just couldn't fall back asleep again.

With a grunt, she shoved the covers back down and stared up at the ceiling. She never should've let them pack the curtains yesterday, she thought to herself bitterly. But they had packed up nearly everything she had owned, getting more of it done than she'd actually expected. They probably could've finished it all yesterday, but Holly had sent them off. She had made the arrangements to drive down to the Archer House today and hadn't wanted to spend last night in a hotel.

Not that staying in her empty house was much better. With so few things remaining, it was practically a ghost town in the place. And without Will or the kids to keep her company, it had been downright lonely. Now, as she lay there trying to wake up, she was actually glad she was heading down to the Keys today.

At least that would give her something to do. And right at that moment, anything to occupy her time seemed like a better option than just sitting around twiddling her thumbs.

By the time she finally crawled out of bed and showered, the sun was fully up. The movers still hadn't shown up, though, not that there was much of a reason for them to be there at the crack of dawn. She had already paid them for the full day, and she would have been surprised if it took them an hour to gather up the remaining things and load them into the moving truck.

No sense in them rushing, especially since everything would just be sitting in storage until she got back from the Keys.

Since she had the place to herself, she took her time leaving, walking around the mansion one last time. This would be the last time she ever woke up in this place, made herself a coffee in the kitchen or host a family get together in the backyard and that thought was enough to bring tears to her eyes. She made sure to stop by each room, savoring those last moments. The kid's bedrooms, their old playroom, the room she had used as a home office, the dining room where they had hosted countless dinners.

There were so many memories in that house. Over twenty years of them, in fact. And Holly wasn't sure what she was going to do without this place. It was strange, knowing even once she finished up in the Keys, she would never be coming back there. By the time she returned, Will would no doubt have moved all of his things out and put the place up for sale. He had lost almost every penny he had when his schemes became public knowledge, and there was no way he could afford this place even if he had wanted to.

No, by the time she returned, there was a good chance some other family would be living there. A happy couple, maybe raising kids of their own. Holly wished that the future owners would have better luck than she had. She'd had some good years, certainly, and she wished them the same, with the added hopes their stay in the house wouldn't end the way hers did.

By the time she loaded her suitcase into the back of the Jag and gotten on the road, her makeup was completely ruined. She didn't care, though. Gone were the days where it mattered if her makeup wasn't perfect. No one back in Islamorada would care how she looked. She would be surprised if any of them even recognized her. It had been so long since she had lived there, and her visit for her father's funeral was very quick.

Thinking about her time in the keys immediately made her think of her siblings. They had been thick as thieves when they were kids. They played together, shared friends, and always had each other's backs. But that had been when they were young. As they grew up, they had all started to drift apart.

No, that wasn't exactly right, Holly corrected. They didn't just slowly move away from each other. They had started fighting more and more, constantly getting on each other's nerves every time they turned around. By the time Holly had moved away for college, she had barely recognized them as the kids she'd once called her best friends.

A lump formed in her throat as tears threatened to fall again. She hadn't spoken to any of her siblings since her father's funeral. And, even then, they had barely said more than was necessary to each other. They had kept things polite and cordial, with respect for their father and grieving mother, but it wasn't the loving and caring relationship they'd once shared with each other.

None of them didn't even have any idea about everything that had happened between her and Will over the last year. Not unless one of her kids had kept in contact with their aunts and uncle, which she doubted. Once she had made a name for herself in realty, it was like her siblings hadn't wanted anything to do with her anymore.

Had Roger called any of them? That lump in her throat grew even larger at the thought of her siblings being there at the Inn. Part of her wanted to see them, wanted to try and rekindle the relationship they'd once had. But the other part of her didn't want to face them. Didn't want them to know what a disgrace she had become.

With any luck, maybe her sisters wouldn't be there. She was pretty sure Randy, her only brother, still lived in town. Last she had checked he still owned his own business at the Bayside Marina about twenty minutes north of the Inn. She probably wouldn't be able to avoid seeing him at the very least.

As if the universe enjoyed toying with her, the Jag jerked and started to swerve slightly. A warning light popped up on her dashboard, a pinging sound echoing through the small car's interior as if she couldn't tell when she had just gotten a flat tire. Holly groaned out in frustration as the car started to slow. She pulled it off to the side of the road as it shuddered to a stop. For a moment, she just sat there, hands tightly gripping the steering wheel and trying to fight back the urge to start banging against it.

Could anything else go wrong in her life? Because, the way

things were going, it was starting to look like a meteor might come crashing down on top of her at any moment. And honestly, she wouldn't have been terribly surprised if one did at this point. Everything else that could go wrong had gone wrong, so why not a cataclysmic event on top of everything else?

Holly closed her eyes and forced herself to take deep breaths. This was starting to become a daily habit for her, she thought with a snort of laughter. If things kept up like this, she was going to end up needing anger management therapy or something.

Maybe going back down to the Keys wasn't such a bad idea. A few days away from all the stress of life might've been just what she needed to really reboot herself. That was if she could ever get there.

As far as she knew, there was a spare tire in the trunk somewhere, but God if she knew how to put the danged thing on. She vaguely remembered her father teaching her and her siblings how to do it years and years ago, but those memories were just phantoms in her mind. Tears stung at the corners of her eyes as she once again resisted the urged to pound her fists against the steering wheel.

She was so close to her destination, too. Couldn't the tire have held out long enough for her to at least get to the Inn? But no, it had to decide to randomly die in the middle of nowhere on the side of the highway. But wasn't that just her luck? Everything that could go wrong this year had gone wrong, so why was she even the least bit surprised at this point?

Pulling out her phone, she stared at it for a moment and then let out a soft sigh of relief. At least she wasn't stranded without any signal. That had to count for something, right?

Thankfully, she also had the number for her insurance saved

into the phone's contact list. But because that seemed to be the extent of her luck, after waiting fifteen minutes to be connected to an actual person, she was told it would take four to six hours before they could get someone out there.

She ended the call in frustration as she blinked away the tears. *I will not have a breakdown!* She told herself sternly. She was stronger than this. No matter how grim or dark things may have seemed, she could muscle through it. She always had, hadn't she?

But if the insurance couldn't get someone out here to fix her car or whatever for hours, what could she do? She didn't quite like the idea of sitting on the side of the road for hours on end, praying they'll show up sooner rather than later. With a sigh, she stared at her phone again.

There was only one person she could call to come to get her out of this mess. Randy.

She'd known she would have to face him at the very least, at some point, but this was not how she had pictured their fated reunion. But what other choice did she have? Uncle Roger was at least in his late sixties. He had no business coming out here to help her change a tire. And Holly wasn't sure what was going on with her mother and didn't want to even risk trying to call her for help.

Which left her with only Randy as her option. Holly smirked as she pictured the look of annoyance that would no doubt be on his face after she asked him for his help. But Randy was her brother. No matter what history the two of them had together, they would always share blood.

And blood helped blood, no matter what. That was one of the lessons her father had drilled into all of them. They didn't have to like each other, but they had to love each other. And while Holly may not have gotten along with her siblings in the last couple of decades, she did still loved all of them, and she had no doubt they loved her too.

So while Randy would be annoyed, he wouldn't leave her stranded out there.

She hoped.

CHAPTER FOUR

Twenty minutes later, a large pickup truck pulled up behind her tiny Jag. Holly's breath caught in her throat as she watched the driver's side door open and a figure hopped out. When the door closed, her chest tightened as her brother made his way toward her car. Even in the mirror, she could see that annoyed look on his face as he shook his head.

Holly risked the slightest smirk, knowing her imagination had been right about the sour look. When she stepped out of her car, Randy stopped a few feet away, and the two of them stared awkwardly at each other. Holly had no idea what to say to her little brother, and it looked like he was equally lost for words.

At least they had that in common.

After a few moments, Randy let out a sigh, and then turned his attention toward the car. Holly may have been mistaken, but she was pretty sure he looked at the car with more admiration than he did his older sister. Finally, his gaze zeroed in on the flat tire on the rear passenger side.

He walked over to it and squatted down in front of it for a moment, looking at it intently. When he looked back up at Holly, he raised eyebrow. "All that money and you still can't change a tire?" he asked dryly.

Holly just shrugged as heat rushed to her cheeks. What else could she do? He wasn't wrong. She didn't think she would ever have to change a tire since the day her father had shown her how. She had always either had Will or someone else to do it for her in the rare event she did had a flat.

"Spare in the trunk?" Randy asked next, and Holly nodded. Before he could ask, she went back over to the driver's side door and pressed the little button to pop it open.

Randy hefted her suitcase out of the trunk with ease, and then lifted the carpet liner to reveal the hidden compartment hiding her spare tire. Holly had known it was in there, but she had never actually laid eyes on the thing. She hoped it was still in good condition, but considering her car was only about a year and a half old, she figured it was a pretty safe bet. Though, with everything else going wrong, it really wouldn't have surprised her if Randy had pulled out a spare tire that was shredded to pieces.

But her luck held this time, and after a few more minutes, the normal tire was off and the small spare was on in its place. Randy stood and wiped the sweat from his brow with the back of his hand and looked at her.

Holly had the urge to offer to pay him for helping her out, but she knew it would just be a futile offer. He'd had the same upbringing she had. You didn't take money from family. You helped them out just because they were family.

"It won't last forever," Randy warned, still all business. In all the time since he had gotten there, he hadn't said anything to her that wasn't related to the job at hand. "But it'll get you to town where you can either get this one fixed or get a new one." He gently kicked the offending tire, then lifted it and brought it over to his pickup truck, tossing it in the back. "I can drop this off at the shop later for you. Doubt you wanna try and squeeze it in the back of the Jag."

Silently, Holly nodded as she stared into the brown eyes of her brother. God, he looked so much like their father that it had almost sent a chill down her spine. Then she thought the tire might fit in there, just barely, but that meant she would have to put her suitcase in the passenger seat. The Jag wasn't exactly designed with storage in mind. But that had been one of the reasons she had gotten it. With the kids grown and off on their own, she didn't need a big SUV that could hold a half dozen kids and their sports gear anymore.

When Randy went to get back into his truck, though, Holly took a step forward. "Wait," she called out, her voice cracking as her heart thundered. Randy froze, one hand on the truck's door, and looked at her. "Why don't we get a cup of coffee or something? Get caught up with each other?"

Holly chewed on her bottom lip as she waited for Randy to respond. For what felt like an eternity, he just stared at her, frowning. Would he just outright reject her olive branch? Or would he at least give her a shot? Finally, he let out a sigh and a half nod. "How about a beer instead?" he countered.

Holly raised an eyebrow, but she didn't comment. It was after lunchtime, at least, so hitting a bar wouldn't be that bad of an option. Besides, if she was going to try and patch things up with her younger brother, she thought a glass of wine mine just be in order. At the very least, it might help the two of them loosen up enough to get passed the awkward silence.

"Sure, that's fine," Holly said, forcing a smile onto her face.

After all, if they were going to sit and talk, did it really matter if it was a coffee shop or a bar?

Just as Holly suspected, as they sat in the old beachside bar that had been there since before either of them was born, things were tense and quiet. Both of them just sipped their drinks and watched each other, only making the briefest of small talk.

God, how had things gotten to this point? As kids, they had always been able to talk about anything and everything. They'd had each other's back and trusted each other implicitly. And now, each time Holly opened her mouth to tell Randy about what a mess her life had become, the words stuck in her throat.

Randy was the first one to even broach anything remotely personal. "How are the kids doing?" he asked, leaning back in his chair.

Holly nodded and looked at her little brother. That was a safe question, at least. "They're doing really good. Both are engaged now, and Sean's baby girl has to be the cutest three-year-old in the world!" Her life may have been a wreck, but she could gush about her kids and grandbaby all day long.

Randy nodded and smiled. "I don't know, Sarah and Emma were pretty cute at that age too," Randy teased with a slight laugh, and Holly laughed alongside him. He had two teenagers, Holly remembered.

She also remembered he had gotten divorced a while back as well. So it wasn't like she was the only one in the family with a failed marriage. And yet, she still couldn't bring herself to tell him the truth. She could see in his eyes he still had this vision of her as the woman who could conquer the world.

She didn't want to shatter that illusion, not for him and not for herself either. Deep down, she knew her dream life was over, but she still didn't want to admit it. To her, if she did, that was like finalizing it once and for all.

They talked about their kids a bit longer, the atmosphere lightening up bit by bit. Now that they had found a safe topic of conversation, and the alcohol had started to loosen them both up a bit, they were both more comfortable sitting at a table together. Even though it had been years since they had done anything like this, It wasn't long before they were smiling.

Finally, Holly had to broach the elephant in the room. "What's going on with Mom and the Inn?" she asked. Roger hadn't given her many details, and she really didn't want to go into the situation blind if she didn't have to.

But Randy just shrugged and took another long sip of his beer. "Don't know. I haven't been to the place in ages. I've got my own business to run and don't have the time to be worrying about the Inn."

Holly peered at him. She may not have been close with her brother anymore, but she could still see right through his lie. She had no doubt he hadn't paid much attention to the family business, but she knew it had nothing to do with worrying about his own business. She could see it in his eyes.

He still hadn't recovered from their father's death. He still harbored his resentment toward their mother. He had always claimed she favored the girls over him, though, Holly knew that wasn't true. But either way, losing their father had been a massive blow to Randy. Even back then, when she'd still had her perfect life and her own things to worry about, she had seen the sunken and hollow look on his face at the funeral.

He looked so much better, at least. His brown hair was a little disheveled. He wore a five o'clock shadow across his chiseled chin and he was pretty fit for a six-foot guy that loved his beer, but she could still see some of the pain in his brown eyes. Holly wondered just how well he had coped over the last two years. And then, she kicked herself for not having kept in touch. She was the oldest, and it was her job to keep tabs on everyone, wasn't it? But even if that was the truth, Holly knew Randy would have just pushed her away if she'd tried to mother him at that point. She'd long ago absconded from her role as the big sister.

The biggest question was, could she ever repair her relationships with her siblings? Only time would really be able to tell.

"Why don't you come to the Inn with me?" Holly suggested. That was where this all started. Shouldn't it be where they rekindled everything?

But Randy wasn't having any of that. He shook his head, his frown deeper than ever. "Thanks, but no thanks. I'm sure you can handle whatever's going on there. You're the successful one out of all of us, aren't you? If there's a problem, you're more than capable of dealing with it." Randy picked up his beer, then downed the rest of it in a single long swallow. "I've gotta get back to work. It was good to see you again, sis. I'll drop that tire off for you."

Holly sat silently as she watched her brother leave. Once the door closed behind him, she picked up her own glass and swallowed the rest of the wine. Even that didn't help fill the emptiness inside her, and she wasn't sure if anything ever would. It was tempting to order another glass and see if that helped, but she didn't want to risk going down that road.

Besides, whatever was going on with her mother and the Inn, Holly was pretty sure she would need her wits about her to handle it, especially since it looked like she was going to be doing it all alone.

Holly sighed and flagged down the waitress to pay her tab. Randy had always been more of a fan of drinking than she was, but something told her she would be back to the little bar at some point. With the headaches she knew lay ahead, she would probably need a drink or two just to stay sane.

CHAPTER FIVE

HOLLY'S NERVES STOOD ON END FOR THE REMAINDER OF THE drive to the Archer House. Even though it had been years since she had last visited, she still knew the way there even with her eyes closed. Not much had changed in Islamadora in her absence. In a way, the town seemed to be frozen in time. And yet, somehow, nothing looked outdated or old fashioned. The town had its own little charm and appeal, which brought tourists there in droves every year like clockwork.

But the moment she pulled up in front of the Archer House, Holly knew why her uncle had called her. The main family house (the Archer House) seemed to be the only thing that had changed. It still stood right where Holly remembered it, but the dilapidated exterior looked nothing like she remembered. The paint was faded and chipped in places. One of the shutters hung lopsided like it was ready to fall at any moment. Even the roof looked like it was overdue for a replacement.

The grounds were a bit better. The grass was at least cut and green, but the flowers and bushes her mother carefully maintained over the years were gone, leaving everything bland and boring compared to how it used to look. God, how long had it been like this? And why hadn't Roger called her sooner?

Was Mom just overwhelmed? Holly wondered as she stepped out of the Jag. She and Dad had split the responsibilities growing up. Had Mom not hired someone to help her out? Was she trying to handle everything herself and getting burnt out? There was no way a single person could handle maintaining this place. Heck, it was always a daunting task for two people!

Holly shook her head, then let out a sigh and headed into the lobby of the Inn. There was a young woman Holly didn't recognize at the front desk, and she grinned cheerfully the moment Holly walked through the door.

"Good afternoon! Welcome to the Archer Inn! Do you have a reservation?" The girl was positively bubbling with energy. Holly froze in place and stared at her for a moment, trying to regain her composure.

"Erm, no," Holly managed to stammer out. She had never felt this flustered before, but somehow the sight of the deteriorating Inn and the woman's unusually perky attitude had her brain a jumbled mess. "I'm looking for Mrs. Archer. I'm Holly, her daughter."

The girl blinked, and then her eyes suddenly went wide. Somehow, it seemed like she was bursting with even more energy than she'd had only a few moments ago. "Oh, my gosh! Your mother has told me so much about you! I feel like I already know all of you so well!" Yep, she definitely had more energy. She looked to be practically vibrating. "Your mother just went to speak with a guest. Room 109. It's... well, I guess I don't need to give you directions! I'm sure you know this place better than I do!"

Holly forced a smile onto her face and gave the woman a polite nod, then headed in the direction of Room 109. The girl wasn't wrong. Holly did know the place inside and out. She had grown up here, helping her parents run the place as a kid. She had helped with housekeeping, gardening, and even ran the front desk as a teenager. All the Archer siblings had had to chip in around the place, each having their own duties.

It didn't take long to find her mother. Holly could hear the irate guest from the other side of the hallway. "I don't care!" the man shouted, his deep, booming voice echoing clearly for anyone who might be around to hear. "I've been here for three days now and the shower still doesn't work properly. I've told you more times than I can count and you still haven't gotten someone here to fix the issue!"

Holly picked up the pace. When she reached Room 109, she found her mother at the entryway. If the sight of the Inn had taken her breath away, her mother's appearance really threw her for a loop. Her skin was sunken and colorless. Her hair was frizzy and dry, hanging loose around her shoulders, so very different from the neatly maintained bun the woman had always worn at the base of her neck.

Uncle Roger had been right. It wasn't just a problem with the Inn being rundown. Her mother was run down, too.

Holly felt her heart break into pieces as she watched the man berate her mother. The older woman looked close to tears. Her entire body was trembling, and if Holly didn't step in and do something, she was afraid her mother might have a breakdown right then and there.

There were other people inside the room, a woman and two young boys. Clearly, they had come here for a family vacation, and Holly could completely understand them being upset over a shower that wasn't working. And considering they were in one of the nicer suites in the Inn, Holly was flabbergasted at just how much her mother had let the place go.

But that was a conversation for another time. First, she needed to put out this fire. Then she could tackle the rest of the issues at hand.

"Excuse me," Holly said, stepping up next to her mother. "My name is Holly Archer. I'm the manager here at the Archer Inn. I want to personally apologize for the troubles you've been having. Our maintenance technician has had a personal emergency and hasn't been able to come in for the last couple of days."

Okay, so most of what she said was a complete and utter lie, but she had to do something to shut this man up before her mother lost it. And the lie seemed to mollify him, at least for the moment. That gave Holly the chance to keep going and try to salvage the situation the best she could.

"How about we move you to another room? One with a working shower. Then you can enjoy the rest of your vacation." Holly smiled at the man, glancing over at her mother for the briefest moment. Her mother mouthed a room number to her, and Holly gave a slight nod. "Room 307 is available. It's a tiny bit smaller than this one, but it has a beautiful view of the beach and ocean. And, of course, we'll be sure to give you a discount on your stay for the inconvenience."

The man mulled over everything Holly said for a moment. No doubt, the word "discount" had gotten his attention. "Yes, that should be fine," he replied, at last, giving the pair of them a quick nod.

"That's wonderful!" Holly clapped her hands together and grinned even broader. This was all a familiar act for her. She had closed enough deals over the years to be able to recreate that same excitement and enthusiasm at will. "Come by the front desk in a few minutes and I'll make sure your new keys are ready. And please, if you have any other problems, just stop by the desk and ask for me. I'll make sure to get anything sorted out for you. Enjoy the rest of your stay!"

Holly and her mother stepped back into the hallway, letting the man close the door. She could already hear him telling his family to pack their things so they could move to the new room. Pushing that out of her mind now that the problem was solved, Holly turned to her mother, who looked almost as shocked to see Holly as Holly was to see the state of everything.

"Hi, Mom," she said, giving her a small smile. She watched as her mother's eyes brimmed with tears, threatening to roll down her cheeks. Holly enveloped her mother in a gentle embrace until her body stopped trembling and then let her go.

Her mother finally looked at her and said, "You're really here. Oh, how I've missed you."

"I missed you too, Mom. We really need to talk," Holly said simply, getting right to the point. Something was going on here, and she was going to get to the bottom of it.

CHAPTER SIX

THE TWO OF THEM STOPPED BY THE FRONT DESK TO INFORM the perky woman of the room change for the guests in room 109; then, Holly led her mother out of the hotel and toward the beach. Neither of them spoke until they were out on the sand, the waves crashing against the shore only a few feet away from them.

They weren't alone out there, not by a long shot. But they had enough privacy to talk without anyone overhearing for the most part. But when Holly turned to face her mother, the older woman looked into Holly's eyes, and then promptly burst into tears. Holly opened her arms and held her mother even as the tears soaked into her blouse.

Her heart, which had already been breaking, completely fell apart. God, how had she let things get this bad? How had she let herself get so sucked into her job that she completely neglected her family? Sure, she had raised and taken care of Gabby and Sean, helped mold them into fine young adults. But she had barely even spared a thought for the family that had helped mold her all those years ago.

It wasn't just her mother she had neglected either. It had been her father before he died, and all of her siblings. When she had left the Keys, she had left them all behind and had barely spared any of them a second thought.

No mattered what had happened that had allowed the Inn to fall into such disrepair; Holly knew she was ultimately responsible for at least part of it. She should've been there. She didn't have to have stayed in the Keys, but she should have at least kept in touch and made an effort to visit more often. She should've been able to see the signs that things weren't right long before they had gotten to this point.

God, if Uncle Roger hadn't called, would she have ever known the truth? Would her mother have called asking for her help?

For what felt like an eternity, Holly just stood there holding her mother. It was the least she could do, all things considered. God only knew how many times her mother had held her over the years.

Eventually, Nelly Archer regained some of her composure. She pulled out of Holly's embrace and took a step back, wiping away tears with the palm of her hand. When she blinked and looked at Holly again, there was a shimmer in her gaze as she looked at her eldest daughter up and down.

"Gosh, I swear you've grown so much," Nelly gushed, her lips curved up into a smile.

Holly chuckled and shook her head. Every time she had come back to visit, her mother said the same thing. Holly highly doubted she'd grown much at all since leaving the Keys at eighteen. No, that wasn't true. She had certainly put on a few extra pounds since then.

No matter what anyone said, you never truly regained the figure you had before kids.

But she didn't bother correcting her mother. Instead, she raked her eyes up and down the older woman, taking in just how much she had aged in the last two years since she had seen her. The poor woman looked closer to eighty than the sixty-nine-years of age she actually was and Holly wished Roger had called her sooner.

"What's going on, Mom?" Holly asked, crossing her arms in front of her chest. She glanced back at the Inn, frowning as she took in its dilapidated appearance once more. The Inn had once been the pride and joy of not just the Archer family but all of Islamorada. Now, it was the one thing in the town that looked like a relic that had been lost to time.

Nelly opened her mouth to respond, then closed it and shook her head. She glanced up at the Inn for a long moment, then turned her gaze back on her daughter and let out a sigh. "Not here. Let's go eat while we talk." She didn't give Holly a chance to argue. She took her daughter's arm and guided her back up the beach toward the small outdoor dining area the Inn had set up for its guests.

Apparently, being the owner and daughter of the owner warranted them special treatment. The head chef came out personally to take their orders, and in no time, they both had gourmet food placed in front of them. That was one thing the Inn still had going for it, at least. The plate of grilled salmon and fresh veggies Holly had ordered made her mouth water just looking at it.

It wasn't until they were both halfway through their glasses of white wine before Nelly finally started to open up about the Inn's woes. "Things have been tough around here since your father's passing," Nelly admitted. She kept her eyes downcast on the plate of food in front of her like it physically hurt to risk a glance up at her eldest daughter. Then again, maybe it did. "Even before your father died, things were tight. We were barely scraping by. Now..."

Holly frowned at her own food. She picked at it aimlessly. It was just as delicious as it looked, but she didn't have much of an appetite. Honestly, she hadn't had much of one since her life started falling apart. It was hard to enjoy eating when everything around her seemed to be crumbling to pieces.

And now that wasn't just a metaphor. Her childhood home, the business her entire family had dedicated itself to at one point or another, looked ready to fall apart at any moment. But while she was helpless to stop her business or marriage from falling apart, maybe she could at least salvage the Inn.

What did she have to lose by trying? She didn't have anything left in Miami. She didn't even have a place to live. She had planned on staying with Sean for a little while, help look after her granddaughter while she tried to figure out what to do with the rest of her life, but nothing had been set in stone.

Holly knew Sean didn't need her there. Not really. He and his fiancé were doing just fine without her help, though they would never turn her away. But here, Nelly did need her help. The entire Inn needed someone's help, and if not her, then who?

Holly set down her fork and looked over at her mother. Nelly still hadn't looked up at her, but Holly could read the shame and embarrassment clear as day. More than that, she felt it. Nelly wasn't the only one who had let things crumble around her, and Holly wasn't going to blame her mother for not being able to stop it.

"I'll stay and help you get everything going again, at least for a couple of weeks," Holly declared. She wasn't sure how much she would really be able to accomplish, but she had to at least try. Maybe if she spent enough time pouring over the Inn's finances and accounting, she could find expenses that could be cut or money that could be reallocated to hiring people to help on a more permanent basis.

Hell, if she had to, she would go out and buy some paint and brushes and start doing some of the manual labor around the place herself. It had been a long time since she'd had to do anything like that, but with some time and a few YouTube videos, she was certain she could turn herself into a regular handywoman.

Nelly's gaze snapped up to meet Holly's. She stared, mouth open like she just couldn't believe the words Holly had just uttered. Not that Holly could blame her. She could hardly believe them herself. After all, she had left the Keys at eighteen, determined never to come back for more than a quick visit.

And, up until today, she had kept that silent promise. But if everything else about the life she had built in Miami was going out the window, why shouldn't her stupid little promises go along with it all?

"Oh, my God, Holly!" Nelly finally exclaimed. She hopped up from her seat and quickly made her way around the table to throw her arms around her daughter. For such a small, frail woman, Nelly sure had a grip still!

Holly fought back a laugh as she hugged her mother back. If she still had that much strength, that had to be a good sign, right? Maybe with Holly there to take some of the stress off her mother's shoulders, Nelly could bounce back physically alongside the Inn. She had to have hope, if nothing else.

When Nelly pulled back, she chewed on her bottom lip,

frowning at Holly. She shifted from foot to foot for a moment, and then let out a sigh. "Are you sure you can? I don't want your business back in Miami to suffer because you're out here—and what about Will and the kids?"

"Oh, it'll be fine and they'll be fine," Holly said, waving away her mother's concerns. She didn't have the heart, or the courage, to tell her mother the truth about Miami. Eventually, she would find out, but Holly wasn't going to rush into that discussion if she didn't have to. No, she would wait until her mother was in a better frame of mind, then sit her down and explain everything. Otherwise, the poor woman might just have a heart attack or a stroke or something, and Holly didn't want that on her conscience. "It's just for a few weeks, after all—just to help figure out how we can get a handle on everything."

The rest of the meal went by in a whirlwind. Nelly was so excited to have her eldest daughter back home that she talked almost nonstop, even after they finished their food. They would have probably sat there all day and night if Holly hadn't convinced Nelly to give her a tour around the property so she could start really getting a feel for all the things that needed work.

And boy, were there a lot of things.

CHAPTER SEVEN

AFTER HOLLY'S TOUR AROUND THE INN AND ITS GROUNDS, they had a small early dinner in the same spot they'd had lunch. Nelly had rambled on almost nonstop the entire time. And, surprisingly, Holly found she didn't mind her mother's constant chatter. It had been so long since she had been to the island; it was actually kind of nice to hear all the local gossip about the things she had missed.

And just like old times, Nelly knew everything that went on in the town. She may have been drowning under the weight of running the Archer Inn by herself, but that didn't mean she didn't always have her ears open for gossip!

Not far from the Inn itself was the Archer house Holly had grown up in. When she caught sight of it, her breath caught in her throat. How many times had she made the journey between their family home and the Inn over the years? More times than she could count, no doubt.

She forced herself to keep walking by Nelly's side, though she desperately just wanted to stop and stare at the place. It was all so much to take in at once, and Holly had a sudden wave of doubt. What was she doing back here, walking toward a place she'd long ago walked away from? What right did she have to come swooping back in to save the day?

What would her siblings say if they saw her now? But despite that doubt, there was one question she knew the answer to that trumped everything else. What would they say if they saw the current state of the Archer House and the Inn? They had cut their ties with the place just as much as she had, but deep down, Holly knew they would have had the same reaction she'd had.

This place had been their home. It held all of their childhood memories and all the love of the Archer family. It had been their father's legacy. They couldn't expect her to just sit back and do nothing, to just go back to Miami and pretend everything was just fine. She couldn't or wouldn't leave her mother like this.

Walking into the house was even worse than seeing it from the outside. The interior had changed very little in the last couple of decades. Even though it had gone from being the home for six people to just being Nelly's, it still looked just as she'd remembered it. Some of the photos on the walls and mantle had changed, been updated to more recent snapshots. But otherwise, it was like going back in time thirty years.

Breathe in, breathe out, Holly repeated to herself. It had become her mantra lately, and it was about the only thing that kept her from having an anxiety attack right there in the living room. Two years since she had been to the house, and even then she had only been in town for a couple of days, staying at the Inn itself, rather than the main house. She'd had Will and the kids with her back then, and it hadn't made sense for all of them to try and cram into the house when the Inn had plenty of open rooms available.

Now, she was planning on staying at the house for at least a couple of weeks. How was she going to manage that, she wondered briefly? There was so much history in this house, more so than even the Inn. She'd had so many milestones and life events in this place, and all of them threatened to come rushing back at a moment's notice.

When Nelly excused herself to head to bed for the night, leaving Holly alone, the younger woman found herself questioning her choice to remain on the island. She left her suitcase in the living room, not wanting to venture up to her bedroom just yet. Just being in the house was almost more than she could handle. Any more than that would take time.

Instead, she headed for the kitchen and found a bottle of wine, pouring herself a glass. She bit back a bark of laughter as she swirled the liquid around in her glass. Maybe Randy wasn't the only one in the family who had a drinking problem, she thought bitterly as she took her first sip. And even if he had been, if Holly wasn't careful, she would be right behind him before long.

Not that that thought stopped her from drinking the glass, then pouring herself another. She'd just taken a sip of it when her phone rang, making her jump and nearly toppled out of the old wooden chair. Closing her eyes and forcing herself to take deep breaths again, she fished her phone out of her too-tight pockets.

When she saw Gabby's name on the screen, she frowned and her heart rate sped right back up. "Hello?" Holly said immediately as she answered the phone.

"Mom!" Gabby exclaimed. Even with the slight distortion from the phone, Holly could hear the panic and apprehension in her daughter's voice. "Where are you? Are you okay?"

Holly blinked in confusion for a moment, wondering why Gabby was so panicked. "I'm fine, dear. I'm at the Inn down in the Keys. Why?"

"Why?" Gabby's voice rose an octave. God, she was so much like her mother, Holly mused. She recognized that tone from many of her own conversations with various people, and that thought brought a smirk to her face. "Sean's here. You were supposed to be at his place today and neither of us have heard a peep from you! Jesus, Mom. You gave us all heart attacks!"

Silently, Holly cursed. With everything going on and Roger's sudden call yesterday, Holly had completely forgotten to tell her kids she'd be down in the Keys checking things out. Rubbing her aching temples, Holly let out a sigh and apologized to her daughter. Then, she did it again when Gabby put the phone on speaker so Sean could be included in the conversation as well.

"Is Grandma okay?" Sean asked immediately. It was as if his anger and annoyance and worry about his mother had faded away in an instance. But that was always how Sean was. He cared more for others than himself. His feelings didn't matter much if someone else was hurting.

"I think she will be," Holly said honestly. "She's just stressed and overwhelmed with everything. The Inn is too much for her to handle on her own without Grandpa. I'm hoping to find a way to take some of the burden off her shoulders so she can take a step or two back and just breathe. Let some other people handle stuff, you know?"

"What about you? How are you holding up?" he asked next. There was apprehension in his voice as he asked the question like he was afraid Holly might just have a breakdown at any slight mention of the turmoil her life had turned into.

"I'm doing okay. As best as can be expected, you know? I'm gonna miss the house and the office and everything, but you know the old saying. When one door closes, another opens. I just gotta stay positive."

She wanted to believe those words, but it was hard to find the positives in everything going on. If they really were there, they were buried deep beneath all the negatives that just seemed to keep piling up all around her. But she wasn't going to say that to her kids. They may have been all grown up now, but they were still her babies. They expected certain things from their mother; being strong and steadfast was one of those things.

"You'll get through it," Sean promised, making Holly smile. Three years of being a father had really changed him. No, not changed him since he had always been kind and caring. Being a father just reinforced those parts of him, and he was always there ready to pick you up when you fell. "We all had some good times in that house, but we'll always have those memories, you know? I bet you missed the Archer House when you moved out, but that didn't stop you from making memories in the new house, did it?"

"No, that's very true," Holly admitted. Sean worked as a contractor, but Holly had always thought he should've become a doctor or a psychologist. He'd certainly had the compassion and a knack for knowing just what to say. She made a mental note to talk to him once she had a better understanding of everything that was falling apart around the Inn. Either she could steer some business in his direction, or at the very least, he might be able to come out for a couple of days if she had to meet with local contractors, just to make sure they didn't try to cheat her.

Gabby's laughter cut through those thoughts. That cackling of hers came through clear as day, even over the phone. "You mean like that time you got your head stuck between the bars of the banister on the stairs?" Holly didn't need to be there to know her daughter would be grinning madly at Sean.

"You're the one who dared me to stick my head between there! I was seven! How was I supposed to know that? Just because I could get my head in there didn't mean it would come back out!" Sean shot back.

Holly put a hand over her mouth to help stifle her laughter as the two of them started bickering back and forth over whose fault it was. It had been terrifying back then, when Gabby had come running to find Holly and Will, giving them the grave news. But now, eighteen years later, even Holly was able to look back on the incident and laugh.

God, the kids, had certainly got up to plenty of antics living in that house! But Sean was right. She'd had the same kinds of memories here in this house and down at the Inn. If they would have asked her back then if she had missed the place, she would have told them absolutely not. But now, with the wisdom that came with age, she knew it would all just have been bluster. She had missed this place like crazy. But that hadn't stopped her from building a life in Miami and creating new memories.

And if she could do it once, what was stopping her from doing it again?

As the kids bickered and went off on tangents into other

memories, Holly slumped against the hard chair. Already it felt like the weight on her shoulders was starting to lift. She still didn't know where she was supposed to go from here, but at least now she had a flicker of hope. If she kept her wits about her, she could begin the slow process of rebuilding her new life.

"So," Gabby said during a lull in the conversation. There was a slight pause after the word, and Holly pictured her kids exchanging a silent glance. "Sean and I have been talking."

"Yes..?" Holly prompted, curious and more than a bit apprehensive about where the conversation was about to take a sharp turn to. With her kids, she never could tell.

Gabby took a deep breath, and then let it out slowly. Either she was holding the phone close, or that had been one heck of a sigh. "We both decided we won't be speaking to Dad again for the foreseeable future. We're not sure if we'll be able to forgive him for what he did. To you, to us, to everyone. And until he does something to prove he's sorry and tries to make it right, neither of us want anything to do with him."

Holly chewed on her bottom lip, struggling to think of what to say in response. She had tried to shield the kids from the brunt of the fallout between her and Will, though it had been impossible to keep everything from them—especially when the true extent of the shady dealings he had been involved with had gone public. It had been front news in every paper for Pete's sake. But while Holly would probably never forgive her now ex-husband, she had never wanted to sour the kids' relationship with their father.

But, at the same time, they were both adults now. They were both fully capable of understanding everything that had happened and made their own decisions regarding all of it. And, from the sound of it, they had spent a good bit of time processing it all. In a way, Holly couldn't blame them. They were well aware of the damage he had caused.

So what could she say? It didn't feel right to praise them for cutting their father out of their lives. But at the same time, she didn't want to say or do something to minimize the effect his transgressions had on everyone.

"Are you sure?" Holly asked, at last, knowing she had to say something.

"We are," Sean answered immediately. There hadn't even been a moment of hesitation from him, which spoke volumes. He was physically incapable of hating or hurting anyone. If he had come to the same conclusion as his sister, then it was likely he'd truly thought it all through.

"Okay. You both know I'm here for you, no matter what, right? Nothing that's happened or will happen can ever change that. You'll always be my babies." Holly took a deep breath, and then let out a sigh of her own. "And despite his faults, I know your father feels the same way. You'll always be his children just as much as you're mine."

The line was quiet for a moment. Holly waited, barely breathing, for what would come next.

"There's something else we need to talk to you about," Gabby said at last. Her voice was apprehensive and uneasy. The tone made Holly shift uncomfortably. The little bit of relief she had felt earlier vanished in an instant. "But, it's better done in person."

"I'm not sure when I'll be back in Miami," Holly admitted, wincing as she said the words. God, she had made all these plans without even thinking to consult anyone else. She had been so focused on not having anything back in Miami she'd forgotten that, just maybe, her kids really did need her. Sure, they were adults, but that didn't mean watching their parent's relationship and careers fall apart wasn't hard on them. "I promised your grandmother I would stay here for a couple of weeks, try and get the Inn back to what it used to be, you know?"

More silence, then another audible sigh. Holly had no doubt it had come from Gabby again, even through the phone. "Okay, but as soon as you know, call one of us, okay?"

"Of course I will," Holly promised.

The conversation didn't last much longer after that. There was a tension in the air; one Holly didn't know how to breakthrough. By the time she hung up, that familiar feeling of helplessness had set back in and she felt a weight on her shoulders once more. It seemed like she just couldn't do anything right. She should have been there for her kids, who obviously did need her.

But she couldn't be there for them and her mother at the same time.

Holly let out a sigh and downed the rest of her wine, then poured another glass. It was going to be a very long night.

CHAPTER EIGHT

MORNING COULDN'T HAVE COME SOON ENOUGH. BY THE TIME Holly had stumbled up the stairs to her childhood bedroom, she had drunk half the bottle of wine. It was more than she had planned on drinking, and if she was honest with herself, it hadn't done much to help the problems at hand. It just numbed them more than anything.

And combined with all the stress, it had led to a rough, sleepless night. Holly had fallen asleep almost the moment her head hit the pillow, but it sure hadn't seemed that way. She had tossed and turned the entire night, and when the sun had finally peaked in around the edges of her curtains, she felt no more rested than when she had gone to bed the night before.

She figured if the sun was up, then she might as well get up. She tried to ignore as much of her room as possible, not wanting to go down that nostalgia trip right then and made her way to the bathroom for a shower. The sleep hadn't helped very much, but the shower certainly had. Just standing beneath the hot spray helped loosen the knots in her shoulders in addition to washing away all the grime from the previous day.

The cup of coffee she made before leaving the house helped even more. There was nothing like some fresh, hot, caffeine first thing in the morning to really get her going. It wasn't a fancy latte or anything, but truth be told, Holly had always preferred just simple coffee.

It was something she'd gotten from her father. If you had even dared to look at his cup of coffee with sugar or milk in hand, you'd end up getting your hide tanned. He drank his as black as possible and wouldn't have dreamed of having it any other way. And that was how Holly had drunk hers for most of her life.

She had learned to enjoy the occasional latte, or whatever fancy concoction Starbucks had come up with that year, but she always had a preference for plain coffee, especially when she was stressed. And today, being stressed didn't even come close to describing how she felt!

Before heading out, Holly had ducked into the room that had been her father's home office. Despite him having been gone for over two years, not much had changed. Nostalgia had once again threatened to overwhelm her the moment she had opened the door, but she had managed to plow passed it long enough to snag a notebook and pen, then flee like the devil himself was after her.

Eventually, she would have to muster enough strength to face all those demons. But there would be time for that later, she told herself. Her personal demons weren't going anywhere. But if she didn't do something soon, the Inn might very well go under. So, for the time being, that had to be her priority.

She had gotten a basic idea of some of the Inn's problems yesterday, but now she wanted to get a detailed look at everything and get it all written down. Then, she could start coming up with a game plan of some sort. What that plan would end up being, she wasn't sure, but again, that was a problem for later!

One step at a time, she told herself.

She wandered the grounds first, jotting things down in the notebook as she spotted them. The grounds were mostly maintained, with the basics taken care of, at least. But it didn't have the same splendor it'd had years ago. Unless they had updated the pictures online, Holly could see why guests might be annoyed when they showed up.

She made notes about the paint, the few shutters that looked loose, and even the parts of the roof that looked overdue for maintenance. Then, it was time for the truly daunting task. As bad as the exterior was in need of some TLC, Holly could only imagine just how much of the interior had been neglected over the last couple of years.

At first, Holly wandered around by herself, just writing down the things that caught her eye. If she noticed them without it being pointed out, then there was no doubt the guests would notice too. And if the guests noticed, then it needed to be fixed as soon as possible. Inns like this lived and thrived on happy customers, and so far, it seemed like at least some of them were pretty far from being happy!

Holly was almost afraid to venture online and see what the reviews said about this place. Eventually, she would have to, though, just to make sure she addressed everything in some manner. But again, that was a problem for another day!

Once she had gone through all four floors and made her notes, she headed back down to the front desk. The same girl from yesterday was there again. Natalie, she had learned, was only eighteen and just out of high school. Nelly had hired her last year to work the summers since Natalie was apparently planning to go to school for hospitality management in the upcoming fall.

When Holly asked Natalie to give her a tour around the place and point out any of the problems, the girl practically squealed with enthusiasm. God, had Holly ever been that energetic when she was that young? She doubted it. And Gabby certainly hadn't been. But Natalie seemed to be bursting with energy and happily led Holly to each of the rooms, pointing out the complaints she had received about each of them.

As it turned out, Room 109 wasn't the only one with a busted shower. Room 302's shower hadn't been working for at least a week either. Those would have to be tackled right away, and Holly instructed Natalie not to rent those rooms out to anyone until she could hire someone to fix them.

Holly went through page after page in her notebook, jotting every single thing down so she wouldn't forget any of it. By the time she returned Natalie to the front desk and headed in the direction of the Inn's restaurant, Holly was already exhausted. Well, more exhausted than she had already been at the start of the day.

And this time, when a waitress brought her a steaming hot cup of coffee, it didn't do much too even take the edge off of things. It was no wonder her mother looked so run down. Holly had only been there for a day, and she was already starting to feel overwhelmed with the sheer size of the project she had agreed to take on.

How in the world was she going to manage to bring the Inn back to its former glory all by herself?

After bringing Holly's coffee out, the waitress seemed to have vanished. Holly looked around for a bit before finally spotting the woman, darting from table to table. Holly sat and watched, and the woman barely seemed to have time to breathe, much less juggle the number of tables she was apparently assigned.

She only spotted one other waitress working as well. So either the rest of them were slacking off somewhere, or they were seriously understaffed. When the young woman finally returned to Holly's table, Holly really took in her appearance this time. Strands of hair had started to escape her tight ponytail. Her makeup was smudged in places, though from sweat rather than tears.

"Is Chef Stevens working this morning?" Holly inquired after giving the woman her order. When the woman nodded, Holly continued. "Can you ask him to swing by my table when he gets a chance? It's not an emergency, so tell him not to rush."

The woman nodded frantically, and then scampered off in the direction of the kitchen. It was a few minutes later when the kitchen door opened and Chef Stevens walked out, a plate containing Holly's food balanced in one hand. He sat it carefully in front of her, giving her a smile as he did so.

"Everything all right, Misses Archer?"

Holly smirked at him and rolled her eyes. The man had worked there since Holly was a girl. Hearing him call her Misses Archer was just too much. "I believe my name is still Holly," she said with a wink. Then, she nodded toward the second chair at her little table. "Do you have a moment to sit and talk? There're a few things I want to ask you."

Chef Stevens frowned but nodded, taking a seat from across the table. The man's shoulders were tense and straight. He met Holly's gaze without blinking. His face was a mix of emotions Holly couldn't quite untangle, but she was pretty sure he was just as stressed and run down as his servers were.

"What's going on with the waitstaff?" Holly asked, figuring it was best to get right to the point.

The Chef's expression hardened immediately. "Pardon?"

"Well, so far as I can tell, you've only got two waitresses to run the entire dining room. And while breakfast may not be as busy as dinner, that doesn't seem like nearly enough people to manage everyone." Holly opened her notebook and got her pen ready. No doubt, she was about to add a few more issues to be sorted out to her never-ending list.

"Well, that would require me to have enough people to properly staff the place!" Chef Steven's snapped. Holly blinked in surprise, not having expected the chef's sudden outburst. Chef Stevens was almost as old as her mother, but he wasn't nearly as frail and meek as she was. "It's bad enough I only have one other person helping me out in the kitchen in the morning. I can't help it if there are only two people out here as well!"

My, God. Were they really that understaffed? That shouldn't have been possible. Pretty much every one of working age in the Keys applied for jobs over the summer every year, especially in places like this. It was a good way for teenagers to earn some extra spending money for the following year or even pay for college if they worked hard enough.

How could Chef Stevens really only be running on two waitresses and a single sous chef in the middle of the summer? The fact that the kitchen was still running at all while being that understaffed was a miracle in and of itself.

But before Holly could say anything of the sort, Chef Stevens stood abruptly. He glared at Holly, and then tossed his white hat onto the table in front of her. "If you think you can do a better job, and then have at it. I've done everything I can!"

Without another word, he turned and stalked out of the dining room, leaving Holly, and the rest of the restaurant, staring at him in disbelief. After a moment, Holly scrambled to stand and run after him, but he was gone before she could catch up with him. Staring at the hat he had left behind, Holly muttered a handful of curses under her breath, then scooped it up and headed into the kitchen.

Just like everything else around the Inn, all four Archer children had spent time working in the kitchen over the years. And while she wasn't nearly as good as a professional chef like Chef Stevens, she at least knew the basics. And since the menu hadn't changed much at all since she was a kid, she still knew how to make each of the various dishes, especially since the breakfast menu was fairly limited compared to lunch and dinner.

Still, Holly had to run around like a chicken without its head to keep the kitchen running without its head chef. While Chef Stevens had complained about only having a single person to help him out in the kitchen, his sous chef was a miracle worker in and of herself. Becky had been hired on only a couple years ago, Holly learned, but that woman knew her way around the kitchen like she had grown up there.

Together, they managed to get all the breakfast orders done and out without many issues. But by the time breakfast was over and the kitchen was closed for a couple of hours before lunch, Holly was barely able to stay on her feet.

Taking a deep breath, she straightened her shoulders. The Inn had many pressing issues that needed to be solved, but the kitchen staffing had just pushed its way to the top of that list. Holly gave instructions to Becky and the two waitresses on getting everything ready for lunch, and then headed out to find her mother.

According to Natalie, she hadn't seen Nelly all morning. Worse, it apparently wasn't unusual these days. That alone sent a chill through Holly. Her mother had always been at the Inn first thing every morning, so had her father for that matter. If Nelly wasn't there, then things were worse than Holly assumed.

It wasn't until she went back to the house and to her mother's bedroom that she found Nelly still in bed. Holly looked at her still sleeping mother and chewed on her bottom lip. She couldn't remember her mother ever sleeping this late, even when she was sick. Part of her wanted to let her mother sleep. If she was still in bed at this time of day, she obviously needed it, right?

But, at the same time, the Inn was falling apart all around them. If they didn't do something, it was going to be too late to salvage it. In the end, her fear of losing the Inn won out, and she woke her mother.

Nelly blinked a few times, and then rubbed at her eyes. "Holly?" she asked groggily. "What're you doing here? What time is it?"

"It's after eleven," Holly said, fighting to keep her voice even and contained. She didn't want to take out her annoyance on her mother, didn't want to place all the blame on her for the condition of the inn. Playing the blame game wasn't going to change the past.

Better to just move on and work toward the future. "I've started making a list of all the problems around the Inn. Let's go into town on a supply run, and I'll give you an update."

Nelly frowned. For a moment, it looked like she might have refused. But in the end, she nodded and began the slow process of sliding out of bed.

Any progress was good news, right? Holly asked herself silently. It was better than nothing, at least.

CHAPTER NINE

ARMED WITH A LIST OF FOOD, CLEANING SUPPLIES, AND ITEMS to start basic repairs, Holly and Nelly piled into Nelly's little Honda. It wasn't the most spacious of vehicles, but it had more room than Holly's Jag did. Plus, Holly hadn't had a chance to make it over to the shop and get the new tire put on yet.

As Holly explained the various things she wanted to tackle first to get the Inn back up to snuff, she noticed Nelly perking up a bit more. It was almost like her mother was starting to find her purpose in life again. And in a way, maybe they both were. On the way to the store, Nelly confirmed Holly's suspicion - she somehow hadn't hired the necessary staff for the restaurant for this summer. She also got Nelly to call Chef Stevens and apologize and promise to get him more staff right away.

It was a little late to be hiring on, but there had to be people out there still looking for work. Or people looking to swap to a different place. That was one thing the island was almost never short on -

people wanting to make a bit of extra cash. The biggest question was how much extra cash did the Inn have on hand? If the appearance of the place was anything to go by, the business probably hadn't been booming.

She made a mental note to sit down with Uncle Roger and go over the finances so she could get a clearer picture of the situation.

Hours went by, but eventually, the two of them managed to get everything on Holly's list. It wasn't everything they would need, but it was the most important things. No matter how badly Holly wished she could just fix everything all at once, she had to prioritize if she wanted to make any progress at all.

"Let's get lunch before we go back," Nelly suggested as they pulled out of the grocery store parking lot.

Holly shrugged, and then nodded. She hadn't gotten to eat very much of her breakfast before she'd had to take over the kitchen, so some lunch was definitely due. They decided on this little cabana-like restaurant not too far away from where they were.

The place was busy since it was right in the middle of the lunch rush. But even with that, they didn't have to wait very long to get a table. Nor did they wait long for a young waitress to come over and take their order. Holly watched the woman carefully, something nipping in the back of her mind. It was like she knew the girl somehow, but considering the girl couldn't have been much older than twenty-two or twenty-three, there was almost no way for Holly to have known her.

At least, not until a few minutes later when the door leading into the kitchen opened and another woman walked out. At that moment, time had grounded to a sudden halt. Melissa. Now it was abundantly clear why the young woman looked so familiar. She'd been the spitting image of her mother, Holly's childhood best friend.

Melissa made a beeline toward their table; a broad grin etched onto her face. "Holly Archer!" the woman squealed, and Holly barely had time to stand before she was enveloped in a bear hug that threatened to break her ribs.

Holly hugged her right back. She was grinning now too, her heart beating rapidly. Just like everyone else she had known in the Keys, she hadn't seen Melissa in years. But God, it felt so good to be with her again, to see the shimmering excitement in her eyes.

"God, Melissa!" Holly gushed, trying to contain her own excitement. She felt a bit like the girl from the front desk right then. "How've you been? What are you doing here?"

Melissa took a step back and laughed. Still grinning, she waved an arm around, gesturing toward the restaurant. "I own the place! Well, alongside my husband. But yeah, we bought it a couple of years ago, fixed it up, and now we've got a booming little restaurant on our hands!"

"Well, good for you! The place looks amazing. And that was your daughter waiting on us, wasn't it?" It didn't seem right, Melissa having a grown adult daughter. But then, Holly had two adult kids of her own. God, where had the time gone?

Melissa nodded eagerly. Holly didn't even have to prompt her before she grabbed a chair and dragged it over to their table. "It is. She's really grown up, hasn't she? And you should see Todd! He's over six feet now. It makes me feel tiny when I stand next to him."

Somehow, Holly had forgotten Melissa had a girl and boy, just like she did. Maybe there was some truth to what Will had said the day before she had left. She really had neglected the people in her life for the sake of her career. It may have been too late to change the past, but dang it, she could still change the future, right?

As it turned out, Melissa only had a few minutes to sit and talk with them. It was a shame, really, since Holly hadn't seen her in so long. She desperately wanted to reconnect with her former best friend and see if maybe she could rekindle the relationship the two of them had all those years ago.

"Hey, we're having a bit of a party tomorrow night," Melissa said as she stood up. She slid her pilfered chair back in front of the table it belonged to, and then turned to face them again. "It's going to be here at the Cabana, but it's locals-only, you know? You should come hang out. I'm sure everyone would be excited to see you again. You know how much we all miss having you around the island."

Holly blinked at her in surprise. How excited would anybody, other than Melissa, of course, be about her returning to the Keys? While she didn't think there was much animosity around town, other than between her and her family, she didn't think anyone else would really be all that overjoyed to have her back.

But with Melissa standing right there, she couldn't very well just tell her no, could she? Besides, what else did she have to do? It wasn't like she could spend every waking moment working on the Inn. Not unless she wanted to become as rundown as her mother had become.

"Sure, I'll be there," Holly said, forcing a smile onto her face. Just because she was apprehensive about the party didn't mean she had to let Melissa know that. Besides, even if no one else cared about her being back in town, at least she would get to spend some more time with Melissa, right? That alone would be worth the effort.

Once Melissa left, though, Holly turned an accusatory glare toward her mother. She had sat there quietly, smiling through the entire encounter, not letting out, so much as a peep. That was all Holly needed to know this had been a set-up. "You knew Melissa and her husband ran this place, didn't you?"

Nelly tried to hide her smile and shrugged. "It must've slipped my mind," she insisted.

Holly wanted to stay mad at her mother. She didn't like being set up. But it was hard to stay angry. Seeing Melissa again, getting to talk to her for a few minutes... It was like she had gone back in time for those brief moments. She had been transported back to before her life had gone to crap.

Sure, back then, she had thought her life was horrible and miserable, but boy had she been wrong. And now, she would have given anything to go back there, to fix things before they could collapse under her.

Before she could say anything else, Melissa's daughter returned carrying plates of food for the two of them. She left them on the table with a wink, and then slipped off to wait on other tables. Holly may not have recognized her right away, but apparently, the young woman had known Holly.

That had to be a good sign, right?

At least, that's what Holly wanted to believe. She needed some hope right about then.

CHAPTER TEN

HOLLY STOOD IN HER BEDROOM, FROWNING AT HER OPEN suitcase of clothes. Why had she agreed to go to Melissa's little party? She barely knew any of the people who would be there. Sure, she would probably remember a lot of them from high school or childhood, but she hadn't kept up with them.

Every few moments, her hand would twitch, itching to pull her phone from her pocket and text Melissa to tell her she wasn't coming. But every time she reached for it, she somehow managed to stop herself. But that little bit of self-control didn't help her figure out what in the world she was going to wear.

"Need some help?" Nelly asked, appearing in the doorway and nearly giving Holly a heart attack. When Holly gave her a reproachful look, Nelly just smirked until Holly relented and nodded.

"I'm not even sure I should be going to this thing tonight."

Nelly waved off her daughter's comments with the flick of her wrist. "Nonsense. You dropped everything back home to come out here and help me. And you've been busting your butt since you arrived. You deserve a night to yourself. Go, have fun. I'm sure Melissa is looking forward to catching up with you."

Holly let out a sigh and closed her eyes. Her mother was right, of course. She had been working almost nonstop since she had arrived in the Keys. A night away from everything just might be what she needed to keep from burning out too quickly. And she was looking forward to seeing Melissa again, too.

Finally, Holly took a deep breath and nodded. She couldn't hide from the world forever. She had to eventually get back out there and interact with people. And what better way to do that than to dive headfirst into a party? At least there, if it got to be too overwhelming, she could come up with some excuse to leave.

Nelly came and helped her pick out a simple sundress to wear. It wasn't going to be a formal party or anything like that, and it was much too hot in the Keys during the summer months to wear anything else. When Holly looked at herself in the mirror, she had to admit she still looked pretty good for being forty-six. She may not have been a young woman anymore, but she certainly could've looked worse!

The moment Holly stepped out of her car in the parking lot she could hear the music drifting up from the beach. There were already a good number of people milling around in the sand. The cabana was lit up, illuminating the entire area even as the sun slowly set on the horizon.

For a long while, Holly just stood there and stared. Laughter could be heard between lulls in the music. Her heart caught in her throat as another wave of panic washed over her. She was tempted to get right back in the car and head home but somehow managed to stay firmly rooted to the ground.

She took a deep breath and closed her eyes, holding it in for as long as she could. When she finally let the air out, she stood with her back straight and shoulders level. She could do this, she told herself. It was just a party with old childhood friends. There was nothing down on that beach she couldn't handle.

At that silent declaration, her body moved on its own, propelling her toward the party. Immediately she started recognizing people, people she hadn't seen or thought of in decades. She hadn't ever come back for any of her high school reunions, and seeing everyone now was like having stepped right back in time.

Sure, everyone had aged, but as she surveyed the crowd of people, it felt just like the parties she had gone to all those years ago.

It wasn't hard to spot Melissa. Holly had expected her to be running around taking care of everything, but apparently, she had the restaurant's staff doing all of that. Instead, she was standing on the beach, drink in hand, talking to another woman. A woman Holly recognized instantly as her other childhood best friend, Chantal.

The tanned skinned woman looked like she hadn't aged a single day in the last thirty-some years. Holly knew she had a daughter, but you'd have never known it by looking at her. Holly only wished she had been that lucky after having her two kids. Because while she may not have looked bad for her age, she looked positively ancient compared to Chan!

The two women spotted Holly only moments after Holly

spotted them. They both grinned broadly and made their way through the crowd before the three of them embraced in squealing laughter.

"Oh, my God!" Chantal cried, squeezing Holly as if she was trying to break her. "When Mel told me you were back in town, I didn't believe her. But here you are, looking like the prodigal daughter returned home."

Holly let out a snort of laughter and shook her head. Chan always had such a way with words. "Nothing quite as dramatic as that," Holly assured her. "Just back for a little while to help Mom get the Inn spruced up a bit. I had no idea she'd had such a difficult time with it after Dad passed away."

"So, you decided to take a break from your big grand life up in Miami to come back and help out, huh?" Chan teased with a wink.

Holly laughed again. Her heart ached as she nodded her head and plastered a smile onto her face. She so badly wanted to tell Chan and Mel the truth, but she couldn't bring herself to do it. Not right then in the middle of a party, especially. This was supposed to be her night to let loose and relax. She didn't want to bring down the mood already.

So instead, she brushed off the comment as best she could with a non-committal "something like that" before shifting the subject to Chan and her life.

As it turned out, Chantal had gotten divorced too. Briefly, Holly wondered if there was something in the water around here that cursed everyone's marriages. But Melissa and her husband were still going strong. Her mom and dad had been happily married right up until the end, too.

So maybe it was just bad luck.

Conversation flowed easily between the three of them as they wandered around the beach. Holly snagged a beer of her own to sip on, hoping it might help mellow out her nerves a little while. After the first sip, though, she nearly spit it out and remembered why she never drank the stuff. Even after all these years, she had never quite acquired a liking to it. And at this point, she doubted she ever would.

But the beer served its purpose. Some of the tension and apprehension she had felt all day faded to the background. It helped that Mel and Chan kept up an almost constant stream of chatter, not giving Holly even a moment to get lost in her own thoughts. It was almost like they knew something was going on and was doing their best to distract her.

"God, I forgot how beautiful it is here," Holly said as the three of them stood just at the edge of the water. It was fully dark now, the only lights coming from the cabana, the moon and stars high above them. Staring out into the ocean, it was like you could see forever.

"No place like it," Mel said with a smirk and a wink. And honestly, that was the truth.

Holly could barely even remember why she had been so eager to leave the place all those years ago. Now that she was back though, her big "rock star" life in Miami having gone up in flames, she wished she'd stayed here like everyone else. She could only imagine what her life would've been like if she hadn't left.

Before she could truly contemplate that thought, strong arms wrapped around her middle and lifted her up into the air. Holly squealed and squirmed, trying to escape her captor's grasp. But no matter how hard she fought, she couldn't get their arms to budge even an inch.

It wasn't until they'd set her back down and Holly whirled around that she realized who had grabbed her. Jason Archer stood there, grinning at her like he'd just won the lottery. He was her eldest cousin, though he was still a few years younger than her. Standing next to him was his brother Paul who grinned just as broadly.

"Well, well, well," Jason said, that smirk seeming to be permanently etched onto his face. "Look what the cat finally dragged back home."

"Jason Archer. Didn't your momma ever teach you not to sneak up on a lady like that? You're lucky I didn't kick you where the sun doesn't shine!" Holly tried her best to sound chastising, but it was nearly impossible to be mad at him. She was still reeling with being face to face with him again for the first time since her father's funeral.

"Eh, it ain't like he uses them any," Paul chimed in. He winked at Holly, and then nudged his older brother. "His wife would probably thank you. Then he wouldn't be chasing her around like a rowdy teen all the time!"

Everyone laughed, even Jason, though he did punch his brother in the shoulder. He may have been able to take a joke, but that didn't mean he wasn't going to remind Paul who the older brother was. Finally, each of them gave Holly a bear hug and told her how good it was to see her back in the Keys.

By that point, Holly was on her third beer, and she was feeling pretty loose and relaxed. Even talking with her cousins didn't spark up her anxiety again, though they also didn't ask too much about her life in Miami. They did fill her in on their lives and the things she had missed over the years, though.

Jason was still happily married to his wife, but Paul and his wife had divorced about a year ago, splitting custody of their two girls. Jason's son, a teenager now, had apparently taken up baseball, and Holly was invited to come to watch him in his next game. Holly accepted, of course, mostly because she was a bit tipsy and it would've been rude to decline.

They were in the middle of talking about his stats for the season when Holly caught sight of a cop heading their way. She froze immediately, her mouth having gone dry. It had only been a couple of days since she had left Miami, but Holly couldn't help think he was coming after her in relation to Will's godforsaken schemes.

But when Jason and Paul caught where her gaze was turned, they grinned and greeted the man with enthusiasm. "Was startin' to wonder if you'd make it out here!" Jason called.

"I came as fast as I could. Didn't even stop to change clothes."

Holly's heart stopped beating at the sound of the man's voice. She knew that voice anywhere. And when he walked closer, she could make out his face. Jake Holton. Of all the danged people to run into at the party, she had never expected to see him.

They had dated in high school, and for a while, Holly thought he was her one true love. But when she had told him about her plans to leave the Keys and work in Miami that had been the end of their relationship. Holly had suggested he come with her, but he had declined, wanting to stay in their home town.

The idea of long-distance wasn't even considered. Back then, Holly had no intention of ever returning to the Keys for more than a quick visit, and Jake had no intention of ever leaving. So they had cut it off, and even though it had broken Holly's heart, she had never really looked back, especially after she had met Will.

But now Will was out of the picture, and Holly was back in the Keys. And there was Jake Holton, looking just as good as he had in high school, standing only a few feet away from her. A man who was no doubt married, Holly reminded herself, but that didn't stop her from ogling just how well that uniform fit him.

He was staring at her, too. She could feel his eyes roaming up and down her body. In just her thin sundress, she suddenly felt exposed as it seemed like his gaze could see right through everything she wore. His lips curved up into a smile, though, and Holly figured he must have liked what he saw. That had to be a good thing, right?

"Well, well, look whose back in town," Jake said with a teasing lilt to his voice. He winked at her, and then smirked again. "And here I thought you would never come back to this little town. What was it that dragged you back this time?"

Holly had just started to explain why she had come back when Melissa interrupted. Her speech was slurred slightly, the drinks hitting her harder than they'd hit Holly, which was probably why the next words had even come out of her mouth.

"Let's go swimming!" Melissa declared. She waved an arm in the direction of the wide-open water. "It's a gorgeous night for it!"

Holly stared at her in surprise. She waited for everyone to dismiss the idea, but to her shock, they all agreed, leaving Holly wondering just how much everyone had had to drink.

CHAPTER ELEVEN

Holly stared in horror as everyone agreed swimming was a great idea. Before she could so much as force out an argument, everyone headed up to the cabana to change into swim clothes.

"I didn't bring a bathing suit!" Holly said to Melissa in a harsh whisper.

Truth be told, she didn't even own a bathing suit. At least, she didn't think she did. Now that she thought about it, she couldn't actually remember the last time she had gone swimming—years ago, at the very least. It just wasn't something that came up very often especially not with how much time she had spent working.

She probably hadn't gone swimming since the kids were little.

Jake laughed from her other side. Holly hadn't even realized he had been standing so close to her still. When she glanced over at him, she saw sparks dancing behind his eyes. "I never pegged you for one to shy away from a little adventure!" he teased.

Heat flooded to her cheeks as a memory came to the front of her mind. It was their senior year of high school. They had snuck out to the docks and onto one of the yachts anchored there. They had spent the night pretending to be a pair of the rich tourists who always flocked to the islands in the summer.

They had gotten up to quite a bit of mischief that night, and even though Holly hadn't thought about it in decades, she could still remember it clearly. And Jake was right; back then, she would have never backed down from a challenge.

And as if all of her old friends were conspiring against her, Melissa piped up next. "Don't worry. I've got an extra bathing suit you can borrow. Come on, Holly, you can't pass this up. When's the last time you went swimming in the ocean under the moon and stars?"

Holly sighed, knowing she was basically beaten. But she still wasn't ready to give up just yet. Holly smirked at Jake, trying one last Hail Mary. "Fine, I'll go swimming, but only if Jake does too."

For a brief moment, Holly thought she might've won and gotten herself out of it. But Jake just returned her grin and nodded, then shrugged his muscular shoulders. "Sure, it sounds like fun to me!"

Holly blinked at him in surprise, which made him laugh. His eyes shimmered, and Holly knew he was taking far too much enjoyment out of this whole situation.

"I've got a set of trunks in the back of my cruiser."

"Have lots of opportunities to swim while you're on duty?" Holly asked, trying to keep her voice neutral. She didn't want him to know he'd beaten her, even if he had.

Jake just shrugged, looking as carefree as ever. "This is the Keys, remember. You never know when you might need them!"

Holly didn't even have a chance to think of how to respond before Melissa dragged her toward the bathrooms to change. Of course, Melissa just so happened to have an extra suit on hand, and one that fit Holly as well. The smirk Melissa and Chantal gave her when she stepped out actually made her blush.

But again, she didn't have much time to dwell on it before she was dragged back toward the water. Before she knew it, there were at least twenty or thirty people out running into the water. The water was warm and soothing as Holly swam out until she was chest-deep.

Everyone around her was laughing and joking around, splashing each other and having the time of their lives. When Jake swam over and splashed her, Holly splashed him right back, and the war was on.

It didn't take long before all thoughts of her crappy year fled from her mind. In a way, it was like she had been transported right back to high school when she didn't have a single care in the world.

Chantal swam over, bumping her shoulder against Holly's. When Holly looked over at her friend, the mischievous smirk was visible even in the low light. She leaned in close, and then whispered her plan in Holly's ear.

Holly's eyes went wide, but she nodded. Jake's comment from earlier had stuck in the back of her mind, and she wasn't about to pass up a chance for a bit of fun. Maybe once the alcohol and adrenaline wore off, she would regret it. She was going to have a bit of fun in the meantime, though.

The two of them swam as quietly as they could. But in the loud roughhousing, their target was none the wiser of their approach—at least, not until Holly and Chan jumped at the same time, both landing on Jake's muscular back. Even as strong as he was, he couldn't hold up the two of them without warning, and he sunk beneath the water.

When he came back up for air, he was sputtering and glaring in their direction. Holly and Chan took a moment to grin and high five each other; then they took off swimming. Jake was right on them though, trying desperately to catch them and exact his revenge.

They split apart, going in different directions. But, of course, Jake chose to chase after Holly. And, of course, Holly wasn't in nearly as good of shape as Jake was, and he caught her before long. She squealed as he plucked her up out of the water like she weighed nothing at all.

Then, before she could even react to how it felt to have his hands on her, he tossed her into the air. Holly yelled again, her limbs flailing before gravity pulled her down into the water with a splash. She sputtered, trying not to inhale the water, as she sunk into the darkness.

When she finally surfaced again, Jake was a few feet away, grinning like a mad man. Holly glared at him, annoyed that it had taken her and Chantal to dunk him and yet he'd been able to send her flying like a rag doll with ease.

Because of course, her high school love had to turn out to be built like a bodybuilder.

Couldn't he have gotten fat? She thought jokingly as she swam toward him for the next round.

CHAPTER TWELVE

By the time the party died down and everyone headed back to the shore to change into dry clothes, Holly was completely exhausted. She couldn't remember the last time she'd had that much physical exertion all at once. But, even though she was sore and tired, she felt good. Better than she had in a while, at least.

Seeing her friends again, letting loose and forgetting about all of her problems that went a long way toward easing some of the stress that had been practically suffocating her. That stress wasn't gone, not by a long shot, but at least for now she could breathe a little bit again.

When she hugged Chan and Mel on her way out, she squeezed them extra tight. She had been really nervous about coming to the little shindig, but now she was glad she had bitten the bullet and joined in on the fun. Not only had she gotten the chance to catch up with friends and family she hadn't spoken to in far too long, but it also helped her rediscover a part of herself she had long ago buried.

Now she just had to try and hang onto that part of her this time.

Walking out to her car, she noticed something amiss almost immediately. Her car wasn't sitting right, and when she reached it and looked at the tires, she wanted to burst into tears. She hadn't gotten a chance to get to the body shop and have the new tire put on her car yet.

And now, sitting right where she left it, was her precious Jag with the spare having gone flat. Why was it, just when she thought things were going so well, the universe had to throw something else at her, just to screw things up again?

One step forward, two steps back. That seemed to be her motto for the year.

Laughter caught her attention. Her head jerked up to see Jake walking out of the cabana, dressed in his police blues again. He was talking with another guy, but after a moment, they went their separate ways. Jake got halfway to his cruiser when he glanced over and spotted Holly, the two of them locking eyes.

He must've seen something in her frantic gaze since he stopped mid-stride, then pivoted to head in her direction. He caught sight of the problem almost instantly and let out a short laugh as he shook his head.

"If it's not one problem, it's something else, right?" Jake teased. His tone wasn't mocking, though, just trying to keep up her spirits a bit. "As if you don't have enough going on with getting the Inn all sorted out."

Holly let out a snort of her own. It was like he had just read her mind. However, he didn't know about the other problems she had been having. Still, she couldn't believe she had never made it over to the body shop to get the new tire on. It was ready. They had called her and told her so. She just had to drive over, pay them, and get it put on.

But of course, that problem had ended up at the bottom of her list.

"Want a ride home?" Jake offered.

Holly chewed on her bottom lip as she considered it. She wasn't so sure she wanted to spend much more time in close proximity to Jake, but what other option did she have? Her mother was no doubt asleep by now. And her cousins had left ages ago.

Sure, she could probably ask Mel or Chan to take her home, but she didn't really want to impose on them either.

So, finally, Holly nodded. "I don't have to ride in the back, do I?"

This time, when Jake laughed, it was a full-bodied one that echoed around them. He grinned broadly at her, and his eyes shone even brighter. "No, you can sit upfront. But if you're a bad girl, I might get out the handcuffs!"

Holly's cheeks flushed with heat at the implication. Quickly, she pushed those thoughts out of her mind and let Jake lead her toward his cruiser. Holly had never ridden in a police car before, and she marveled at the layout.

"So, how's life in Miami?" Jake asked as they cruised down the highway. He glanced over at her; his curiosity was more than evident in his eyes.

Holly shrugged, fighting to keep her expression neutral. She still hadn't gotten the courage to tell anyone about her life falling to pieces, and this still didn't seem to be the right time to do it. "Really good. Me and Will are very happy. The kids are doing better than ever."

"I'm sure they miss you terribly. How old are they now?"

"Gabby just turned twenty-six. Sean is twenty-five now, with a three-year-old daughter of his own."

Jake nodded. His attention was firmly on the road ahead of him, his hands gripping the steering wheel tightly. Somehow, the relaxed demeanor from this evening had slipped away. "They grow up so quickly, don't they? Mine are eleven and thirteen now, and I swear it was just a few weeks ago they were still crawling around in diapers."

"I didn't know you had kids," Holly said, her eyes wide. She hadn't noticed a ring on his finger, and he hadn't mentioned anything about being married or having kids earlier.

But then, neither had she. The conversations all night had stayed light and surface level. The only really intimate things they talked about were things from their pasts, shenanigans and hijinks they had gotten up to in their youth.

"Yep. A boy and a girl. They live with their mother in Naples." Holly didn't need to look at him to know how much that hurt. She could hear the pain evident in his voice. He must have missed his kids terribly.

"How long have you been divorced?" Holly found herself asking. Then, she mentally chastised herself. It wasn't any of her business. And if she didn't want people prying too deeply into her personal life, didn't they deserve the same respect from her?

But Jake just shrugged. If the question bothered him, he didn't show it. "It's been a couple of years now. Three? Four? I don't know. It's been long enough."

Holly nodded silently. He didn't sound too broken up over his divorce. Maybe time really did heal all wounds? She thought to herself. Maybe in a couple of years, she wouldn't feel a stabbing pain in her heart every time she thought about Will or the kids or the life she'd had back in Miami.

Before Holly knew it, they were pulling up in front of the Archer family house. She forgot just how close everything in town was. Unlike Miami, it didn't take an hour just to go a couple of miles.

"How about you?" Jake asked as Holly opened her door and stepped outside. She bent down to be eye level and looked at him with a furrowed brow, confused with his question, and he clarified. "How long have you been divorced now?"

Her heart stopped beating. Wide-eyed, she had stared at him. She hadn't told anyone, so how could he have possibly known? Besides, she had just told him things were going great, hadn't she? "I don't know what you mean. We're both happily married," she forced out, plastering a fake smile onto her face.

But Jake just chuckled. He looked at her, the two of them locking gazes. It really was like he could see right through her. Even after all these years, he still knew how to read her. "If that's the lie you're going with, you might wanna start wearing your wedding ring."

Holly stammered out a response as she quickly closed the door. Jake looked at her one last time, and then slowly headed back down the driveway. Her cheeks were flushed with heat from the embarrassment of having been caught in her lie.

Jake probably thought she was pathetic, lying about her life still being perfect. But as she stood there under the moonlight, she could still see the look he had given her. Whatever he'd been thinking, that hadn't been it. But no matter how long Holly pondered, she couldn't quite decipher what he had actually been thinking.

She couldn't quite read him as well as he could read her.

CHAPTER THIRTEEN

H<small>OLLY WAS SITTING AT THE FRONT DESK, TALKING WITH</small> Natalie, when the two trucks pulled up out front. The younger woman looked at her curiously as Holly grinned and jumped up from behind the desk to head outside. She had just crossed through the glass door when the passenger door of the truck opened, a woman sliding effortlessly onto the pavement.

"Cara!" Holly exclaimed, rushing over to embrace her cousin. Cara was Jason and Paul's little sister. Even though she was thirty-eight now, she looked like she had barely aged a day. What was it with the people around here not seeming to age? Holly wondered bitterly.

"Oh, my God, it's so good to see you again!" Cara hugged her back, but at least she didn't try to break her in half like everyone else was prone to do. "When the guys told me they were coming by to help spruce up the Inn a bit, I figured I would come along and lend a hand. The Inn may have been your father's pride and joy, but I'm still an Archer too."

"I will take all the help I can get! But first, you and I need to do some serious catching up while the guys look over the place and make out a plan for us." Holly left them with the notes she had taken and they made arrangements to meet up at lunchtime to go over everything together.

Then, Holly hooked her arm in Cara's and guided her cousin down toward the water. It was another beautiful day, with the sun high above and barely a cloud in the sky. You could smell the saltwater in the air, and that alone was enough to ease even the worst stress.

"So, how's life been treating you?" Holly asked. After so long of being cut off from everyone she had grown up with, now she had almost an addiction when it came to getting caught up. She was almost as bad as her mother, needing to know what was going on and what she had missed.

Cara shrugged, and then reached her arms high up in the air to stretch. "As good as I can hope for, I guess. Did you hear Greg and I got divorced?"

"No, I didn't. When?" Holly was starting to see a pattern. She was pretty sure she now knew more divorced people than married ones!

"About a year and a half ago. It just wasn't working out for us. We spent more time fighting than anything. Once we separated, we started getting along much better."

"Well, I guess that's good," Holly said, trying to be careful with her words. Just because Cara seemed relaxed about her divorce didn't mean Holly could be careless with what she said. "How's your daughter handling it? She's what, fifteen? Sixteen?"

"Sixteen," Cara confirmed. "And she's been doing good too. I think she's happier now that her father and I aren't fighting all the time anymore. The two of them are actually on a trip right now. They wanted some daddy-daughter bonding time before school started back up."

"Ah, so that's why you really tagged along with your brothers. You just wanted to use me to ease your loneliness," Holly teased with a smirk. As they walked along the shore, carrying their shoes and letting their feet dig into the sand, Holly couldn't believe she had stayed away for so long. She had missed so much by never really coming back, and she wasn't sure she would ever really be able to repair those mistakes.

Cara laughed and nudged Holly with her shoulders. Cara's blue eyes were almost the same color as the ocean, the sun making them sparkle. "Well, you have to admit, walking along the beach with you is better than being holed up in my studio all day!"

"How's the art going? Are you the next Picasso yet?"

"God, I wish! That was actually one of the things Greg and I always fought about. Having two artists in the same house just wasn't working. Our incomes are too hit and miss to really be comfortable, especially with a teenage daughter, you know? And then with the stress on top of everything, it just made our work suffer. Things are bouncing back now, though, and my little apartment is much easier to afford than the big house we had all been sharing."

"Well, we'll have to talk to the guys. Not much of the interior of the Inn has been updated in decades. Maybe we could use some of your art to help breathe a bit of new life into the place." Holly still hadn't gotten a chance to do a deep dive into the Inn's finances, so she had no idea how practical the idea was, but she figured she could make it work one way or another.

Family had to stick together. She had learned that much, at least since returning to the Keys.

Cara cackled and gave Holly a wicked smirk. That was a look Holly had seen on her younger cousin many times over the years. It usually meant some sort of chaos was about to follow.

"I like the sound of that! And I've already got some pieces I think would look great around the place." Holly could see the gears turning inside her cousin's head as she started making plans. She had spent almost as much time at the Inn growing up as Holly had, so no doubt she knew the place inside and out. "Are the paintings in the rooms themselves still the same? Because if so, we really need to update those. They were just cheap, mass-produced ones anyway. Having art from a local artist would be a good selling point too."

Holly smiled as she listened to Cara ramble. Cara really wasn't talking to her anyway, just getting her thoughts out to help make sense of them. Holly did the same thing sometimes, especially when she was getting overwhelmed and really needed to sort everything out mentally.

"So, how about you? How's life in Miami been?" Cara asked a little while later, once she had worked through her little planning session. Even before talking to her brothers, she already had the entire thing planned out!

Blinking at Cara, Holly felt her heart rate picking up again. As her cousin looked at her, waiting for an answer, Holly couldn't figure out what to say. She should tell her the truth, shouldn't she? Eventually, everyone would have to know. This wasn't a secret she could keep hidden forever.

Besides, Cara would understand. She had been through a divorce herself. And even if hers was a bit more amicable than Holly's, she understood what it was like to have your marriage and life fall apart around you.

And yet, Holly couldn't make the words come out, no matter how hard she tried. They just sat there, stuck in her throat, refusing to budge.

Then, her phone rang, and Holly let out a sigh of relief. At least she had a temporary fix to her problem, though she knew it would still be waiting there after her call. When she glanced at the number, though, she frowned. It was the number for the front desk at the Inn.

Had the guys finished early? Or had they found a major problem that needed to be fixed right away? No, that didn't make sense. If it was one of them that had needed her, they would have called her on their cell phones, not from the front desk.

Holding her breath, Holly answered the call. "Holly Archer," she said automatically.

"Holly, oh thank, God! I wasn't sure who else to call!" Natalie said her voice more frantic than Holly had ever heard it.

"Easy, Natalie. Take a deep breath and tell me what's wrong." Holly stopped walking and closed her eyes, taking slow, deep, breaths herself. Whatever crisis had popped up this time, Holly was sure they could handle it.

She heard Natalie's deep breathing over the phone, and when she spoke again a few moments later, she sounded a bit less frantic.

"It's your mom, Holly. She was in the office going over some paperwork when she collapsed."

Holly's heart had been racing before, but now it felt ready to burst from her chest all together! She had known her mother hadn't been looking great, but now she had collapsed too? Her health issues must've been even worse than Holly had thought.

"Call an ambulance. We'll be there in a couple of minutes." Holly ended the call, then stuffed the phone back into her pocket and took off running toward the Inn. Cara, having only heard Holly's end of the conversation, followed along right beside her.

As they ran, Holly filled her in on what Natalie had said. Cara's eyes went wide, and Holly saw the same panic on her face that she felt inside her.

One step forward, two steps back.

CHAPTER FOURTEEN

Holly's entire body seemed to shake as she paced back in forth in front of the row of chairs. All of her muscles were wound tight, and her impatience grew with each passing moment.

The ambulance had rushed her mother to the hospital. She and Cara had followed right behind with Paul and Jason in tow. Now, the four of them were stuck in the waiting room, hoping the doctor would come to pay them a visit sooner rather than later.

Her mother had been conscious when the ambulance had driven her away, so that had to be a good sign. Maybe she had just gotten overheated or something with a similar fix. Maybe she had just been dehydrated. Holly could make sure her mother drank more water every day if needed.

The guys sat in the hard plastic chairs, somehow not nervous wrecks. Cara was pacing along with her, though, so at least Holly wasn't the only one who was ready to have a nervous breakdown at any moment.

The entire time, Holly kept thinking about how different things might have been if she hadn't stayed away for so long. Even if she had just come back more often after her father had died, maybe she could've stopped this before it had even really gotten started.

There was no way for her to deny the fault landed squarely on her shoulders. She was the oldest child. It had been her responsibility to make sure her mother was okay, and she had completely dropped the ball on that duty.

God, how was she ever supposed to live with herself after this? Just stopping by for a couple of weeks to spruce up the Inn wasn't going to be enough. She had to do more. She had to figure out some way to make sure her mother was taken care of and the Inn didn't just start deteriorating the moment she left.

Her phone rang as she paced up and down the row of seats. A quick glance at it showed her daughter's picture, and Holly sent the call to voicemail. With everything going on, she just couldn't talk to her right then.

If she did, Holly wasn't sure she would be able to contain herself. And while she had no doubt she would have a breakdown sooner or later to get all of her emotions out, the middle of a hospital waiting room wasn't the place for it. She had to keep herself together at least until she knew her mother was okay.

She could do that much, couldn't she?

Gabby called a few more times while Holly waited for the doctor, but she ignored each call. Every time she saw her daughter's face, a pang of guilt stabbed her right in the heart. Part of her felt guilty about not answering the calls, but with her mind racing and the panic really starting to set in, Holly doubted she could focus on anything Gabby said. And that was assuming she didn't have a breakdown.

Holly would call her back, she promised silently. Once everything was squared away, she would make time for whatever it was her daughter needed. But, until then, she had to devote what little attention span she had left to her mother.

When the doctor finally appeared in the doorway of the waiting room, Holly almost collapsed with relief. She rushed over to him, eager to find out what his diagnosis was, praying she would be able to take her mother home.

"Your mother is extremely fatigued," the doctor said, jumping right in and not mincing his words. "She hasn't been eating properly. Her weight is down considerably, she's been dehydrated for a while at least, and if something doesn't change soon, she's liable to have a stroke or worse."

Holly's mouth went dry as she listened to everything the doctor said. Deep down, she had known all of this already. She'd known it the moment she had laid eyes on Nelly that first day back at the Inn. But she hadn't realized just how bad things had gotten.

"She's also extremely depressed," the doctor continued. "Which would explain a lot of the problems. I'm going to write her a prescription for some medication, but she's going to need to see a doctor regularly to maintain it. And I want to keep her for at least a night or two, just to make sure she's stable. Keep her on IV fluids and eating to rebuild her strength. Then, she should be fine to go home, provided she makes the necessary changes to her diet."

Mutely, Holly nodded. It sounded like it was going to take more than just sprucing up the Inn and getting it back on track for her mother to see any improvement. She was going to need a lot of rest and someone to keep an eye on her.

"How long do you think it'll be before she's one hundred percent again?" Holly found herself asking, needing to know upfront. She couldn't keep her head buried in the sand anymore. Whatever problems were going on, she needed them out in the open. She needed to face them head-on.

The doctor paused and frowned, thinking the question over. He looked at the clipboard he carried, flipping through a few pages, no doubt reviewing Nelly's chart. "Other than the severe fatigue caused by the depression, she's in pretty good health. A month or two of taking it easy, eating and drinking like she needs to, and she should be on her way to a full recovery. And if she really takes this seriously, there shouldn't be any lasting side effects, either."

Again, Holly nodded. A month or two, at least. And that was just to get her on the road to recovery and out of the danger zone. It was going to take even longer for her to fully get back to her old self.

And there was no way she would be able to run the Inn and take it easy at the same time. That meant someone else would have to step in and take over the fulltime operation of the place, even if it was only temporarily.

After the doctor left, Holly gave her cousins the news. They all relaxed a bit, but Holly could see the concern in their eyes, alongside the guilt. They had been here, they had seen the state the Inn had been in and knew Holly's mom hadn't been looking great, and none of them had done anything about it until it was too late.

Holly didn't blame them, though. There was only one person she blamed, and that was herself. She had purposely cut herself off from her family and everyone else in the Keys, trying to chase an unsustainable lifestyle in Miami.

It wasn't their fault the Inn had fallen apart. Sure, they were Archers, but they were only related to her mother through the marriage to her father. Nelly wasn't their responsibility. They had their own issues to deal with, their own families to focus on.

This issue was Holly's, and the blame rested squarely on her shoulders.

Sitting around feeling guilty wasn't going to solve anything. As Jason drove her back to the Inn, Holly made up her mind once and for all. If someone had to take over the Inn and care for her mother, it needed to be her.

This was her responsibility. And now that there wasn't much left for her in Miami, there wasn't any reason for her not to stay here. Whether it took two months, six months, or a year, Holly was going to make sure everything was right, one way or another.

Jason looked at her with surprise when she told him her decision. Then, he smirked and nodded. "Well, everyone else may have given up hope of you ever returning, but I always knew the truth. You couldn't stay away from this place forever. You are an Archer, after all."

CHAPTER FIFTEEN

Sitting at the dining room table, Holly stared at her phone. She knew she needed to call Gabby back still, but she figured she should call her siblings first. After all, if their mother was in the hospital, they deserved to know about it. She would have wanted someone to call her if she had been in their shoes.

Dialing their numbers, on the other hand, was much harder than just thinking about it. In the end, she opted to call Randy first. She had already scratched the surface of the ice between the two of them, at least, so she figured he would be the least likely to bite her head off.

In fact, he sounded almost jovial when he answered the phone. "I hope you're not stuck on the side of the road again. Otherwise, I'm going to have to charge you like a taxi would," he teased.

Holly snorted and rolled her eyes. Even if she had been on the side of the road again, he would've come and gotten her, just like he had done the first time. "I wish. At least that would be an easy fix."

"Okay, then what crisis has you calling me this time? Because I know you didn't just call to chat."

There was an edge to his voice. Maybe if she had called just to chat once in a while over the years, this conversation would have been easier. But while her cousins may have forgiven her for running off practically the day she turned eighteen, her siblings still hadn't.

"You should see this place. You remember how it was when we were kids. Dad never let so much as a scratch on the walls linger for more than a day. Now... it's a wonder the place is still standing."

Jason and Paul had given her a rundown on the things they'd figured out before Nelly had her incident. And while she remembered some of it, most of it had gone in one ear and out the other. She hadn't been in the right frame of mind to actually listen to what they'd been saying, even if it had been a good distraction from everything for at least a few brief moments.

What she did remember was the sheer scope of this project. It definitely wasn't a weekend of hard work. It was going to take a couple of weeks, if not a month or two, to really make the place shine again. And while she knew Jason and Paul wouldn't even think twice about pitching in, she couldn't expect them to do it all. They would need to bring in their crews, and those crews weren't going to work for free, nor would she ask them to.

"Dad's probably rolling over in his grave," Randy replied. He tried to sound amused, but Holly could hear the pain in his voice still. This place had been Dad's pride and joy. It probably killed Randy to see it falling apart just as much as it killed her, maybe even more so because of just how close he had been to their father.

"I doubt it. You know him; he always took everything on

himself and never held a grudge against anyone." Holly smiled at the memory of her father. He'd always been a good man. If they did something wrong, he would chastise them, but he'd help them do better next time. And he wasn't afraid to admit when he had made a mistake. "But the Inn isn't the problem. It's Mom."

"What's wrong?" Randy's voice changed again. Now, there was no sign of the lightness. He didn't even pretend.

"She's in the hospital. The doctor says she's severely depressed and hasn't been eating or drinking enough. She collapsed today, and they're keeping her for a couple of days just to make sure she's okay."

"Jesus," Randy said at once. Then, he was quiet for a moment, and Holly wondered just what was going through his mind at the news. "She'll recover, though?"

"The doctor thinks she will, provided she gets some rest and starts eating better. You should come out and see her, though. I'm sure it would help get her spirits back up."

"I doubt it," Randy shot back immediately. "You know I was always her least favorite. She always preferred you, girls, over me."

Holly bit her tongue, wanting to argue on her mother's behalf, but it seemed pointless. Randy had made up his mind about his treatment long ago. Nothing she would say now would be able to change that.

"You should still come to see her."

Randy was quiet for a moment. Well, more like a minute than a moment. Holly had to check and make sure he hadn't hung up before he finally responded. "Let me know if she gets any worse. If she does, then I'll see about coming down. But otherwise, I've got work to do."

That time, Randy did hang up, before Holly could even say goodbye. She sighed and slumped down in her chair. If that was the easy call, then she was definitely not looking forward to calling her sisters.

But she did. It took her a couple of minutes to build up the courage, but she tapped on Rina's name in her contacts list. Then, she held her breath as the phone rang, wondering if her sister would even answer.

They were only a year apart. As kids, they had been best friends. They had done practically everything together. But as they had approached their teen years, things had quickly changed. It was like they were constantly at odds with each other.

Usually over boys, if Holly recalled correctly. Being so close in age, they often sought the same guys. And when they were both interested in the same boy, there was no outcome that could please both of them. And there was only so much tension and arguing a relationship could handle, even one between sisters.

The line connected, but there was silence for a minute. Then, Rina's distinct voice came over the line with a single word. "Yeah?"

"Hey Rina," Holly said, forcing a neutral tone into her voice. If this was how they were starting off, Holly didn't want to give her sister any more ammunition than she already had. "It's Holly."

"Yeah, I know. What do you want?"

Yikes, Holly thought. Rina was not in a very good mood it seemed, though Holly hadn't actually expected her to be. It was why she had called Randy first, after all.

"Mom and the Inn aren't doing well. She's in the hospital and the place is falling apart." No sense in dancing around—might as well just get straight to it.

Rina snorted. Holly envisioned her rolling her eyes. "So, what, you decided to swoop in from your fancy life and save the day?"

"No, it's nothing like that. I just don't want to see the family Inn falling apart. Nor do I want our mother working herself into an early grave. We already lost Dad. I don't want to lose her too."

"What did the doctor say?"

She listened quietly while Holly relayed everything the doctor had told her. Then, she sat and waited for Rina to respond. Randy hadn't been eager to come back home, but that was because of his own issues with Mom. Maybe Rina would be more agreeable since she didn't have that same decade long tension.

"Well, then she'll be fine. You're there to take care of her, so what more could she need? I'm not gonna drop everything in my life just because she needs to eat better."

"Jesus, Rina. This is our mother we're talking about," Holly said, at last, unable to hide just how annoyed she had gotten. "Is it really that big of a deal for you to come see her for at least a couple of days?"

"Oh, please, Holly. Stop trying to be the martyr! You're there already."

"What the hell is your problem? Our mother is lying in the hospital and the Inn we all grew up taking care of is literally in tatters. So why are you acting like this?" Holly's anger had bubbled to a boil now, and she didn't care much about antagonizing her sister anymore. If she was going to act like a brat, then Holly was going to treat her like a brat.

"If you really must know, Dennis died six months ago. So excuse me if I'm not going to go rushing back home when you know damn well everyone in the family hated him!" Rina snapped. Her voice had risen to the point she was shouting into the phone. "So there, that's why I'm not coming back, since you just had to push the issue. So please, do us both a favor and don't bother calling me ever again!"

The line went dead a few seconds later, and Holly stood there, mouth hanging open, trying to figure out how the call had managed to go that badly. She hadn't been expecting sunshine and rainbows, but she hadn't been expecting that, either!

Setting the phone down on the table, Holly just stared at it. She was still in shock over her sister's sudden outburst. Not that she was upset or angry, but the fact that her husband had died months ago and she hadn't told anyone.

Not that Holly was much better, since she hadn't told anyone about her divorce and everything else. But at least Will was still alive! Jesus. And her two sons. Holly couldn't even imagine what they all must have gone through or still be going through. She could feel the lump in her throat threaten to choke her and she felt a little nauseated at the thought.

Even though coping with a divorce was tough. How was Rina coping with the death of her husband? That was almost infinitely worse, and from the sound of it, she was going through all of it alone with her boys. Sure, she probably had friends helping her out, but wasn't that what family was supposed to do?

Once again, that familiar stab of guilt hit her, knocking the air from her lungs. She had messed things up again, this time with her sister. She should have reached out to Rina years ago, tried to patch things up between them. They were sisters, for crying out loud! Letting teenage rivalry get between them for so long was just insane.

And yet, she had been so absorbed in her new life; she hadn't even considered how everyone else might be doing. Now, there she was, with another ruined relationship, and this one, she honestly had no idea how she could ever repair.

Heck, it didn't even sound like Rina would ever even want to try.

Holly still needed to call Amy, Randy's twin sister, and tell her the news. But after how the last two calls had gone, she just didn't have the heart or energy to do it. Two catastrophic phone calls in a single night was all she could handle. Anything else would just end up being the breaking point.

She would eventually have to call Amy. It wouldn't be right not to at least try to let her youngest sister know what was going on. But that could wait, she decided. It wouldn't do anyone any good for her to have a breakdown over the phone. If anything, it would just make everything worse.

Somehow, she had to hold it together. Nelly needed her in one piece, needed her to be the strong one now. And after everything her mother had done for the family over the years, this was the least she could do in return.

CHAPTER SIXTEEN

RUNNING A HAND THROUGH HER HAIR, HOLLY WISHED SHE had a hairbrush on her. She had done the motion so many times that morning she'd managed to get tangles in her dark brown hair. Nothing a good brushing wouldn't get out, but since her hairbrush was back at the house, she would just have to wait until later.

Besides, unless something suddenly changed in the books in front of her, she was just going to keep repeating the habit over and over again. It was something she had started doing as a kid, and no amount of stress balls or fidget items had ever been able to cure her of it. When she got stressed, she started playing with her hair.

And boy was she stressed.

She was in Nelly's office at the Inn, finally sitting down and going over the accounting books. The Inn may not have been in its prime at the moment, but it still should've been bringing in more money than it was. Summer had always been busy enough to keep them afloat for the entire year. There was no reason her mother shouldn't have been able to hire people to help ease her burden.

Except, the money didn't seem to be there. It should've been there. The Inn had been solidly booked; as far as Holly could tell, the accounts should have reflected that. But they didn't, and no matter how many times Holly went over page after page of numbers, they just didn't seem to be adding up to her.

Finally, she picked up the office phone and called her cousin Roger who managed most of the Inn's accounting. He answered on the second ring, and unlike the last time she had called a family member, he actually sounded pleased to hear from her.

They made small talk at first, and Holly filled him in on everything with her mother. Roger promised to come visit her and check on her soon, which was more than anyone else had done. But then, Roger was one of her mother's closest cousins, and he had always kept an eye on things.

"Now, since you're calling me from the office and not your cellphone, I'm guessing you didn't intend for this to be a personal call?" Roger teased.

Holly smirked. He was so much like her mother. He knew how to be polite when needed, but he wasn't afraid to cut the crap either. And when it came to running a business's finances; that was the exact attitude he needed. "I'm going over the books for the Inn's finances, but it's not adding up or making sense to me. As far as I can tell, we've been booked pretty solid for the last couple of months. Maybe not sold out like we used to be, but more than enough to get by. But it doesn't seem like the money's all there?"

"I've been wondering that myself," Roger admitted. "I go over everything multiple times, and every penny seems to be accounted for, but the account balances aren't growing like they used to. Nelly kept assuring me everything was fine, but numbers don't lie."

"Now I see why you called me," Holly said as she ran a hand through her hair again. Money was missing from somewhere. All the books added up, which meant something was happening to it before it got logged. If the money didn't get logged, then it wouldn't be noticed if it went missing. But how was money not getting logged? And where was it going?

Roger and Holly went over some of the numbers together. And, like he said, everything added up—except it didn't. Not when Holly pulled up the booking information from the last couple of months. With how many rooms they had sold each night, their recorded income should've been a lot more than what was reported.

Was Nelly's depression to blame? Holly wondered. With all the stress and fatigue, had she somehow mischarged people? Or spent the money on things and forgetting to properly log it all? She shared her thoughts with Roger, and he was just as stumped as she was.

"It's not like this is Nelly's first year running the place. You know as well as I do she handled more of the backend of the Inn even when your dad was still alive. Keeping the books and managing everything was always her strong suit. I can't see her making massive mistakes like this, not unless there's more going on with her than just depression and fatigue."

Holly agreed. A couple of mistakes here and there, Holly could understand in light of the current circumstances. But this was more than just a couple of mistakes. And as far as Holly could tell, it went back more than just a few months too, though she hadn't gotten a chance to go too far back into the books.

Holly turned the office chair so she could stare out the window as she spoke with Roger. Even between the two of them, they couldn't quite figure out where the money had gone. It obviously hadn't been used to maintain the Inn. Nor had it gone to hiring more staff.

So where was it?

Holly's mind kept going around in circles, not getting her anywhere. She opened her mouth to say something to Roger, but the moment she did, that thought slipped right out of her mind. Instead, she focused on a man walking across the property toward the pier that held their boathouse at the end of it. They used to store all the water toys and other items for the Inn when they would take out guests on water excursions.

Leaning forward and squinting, Holly tried to make out who the man was. But, try as she might, she didn't recognize him. As far as she knew, he wasn't one of the Inn's employees. And if that was the case, then who was he? And what was he doing heading out to the end of the pier toward the boathouse?

"I'll have to call you back," Holly told her uncle. As much as she wanted to get to the bottom of the Inn's finances, this was a bit more pressing. If someone thought they could sneak around in broad daylight and steal from them, they were about to get a good shock.

Cell phone in hand, Holly headed out there. She probably should have just called the cops right from the office, but with her luck, if she had done that, it would had ended up actually being an employee she either hadn't met or hadn't recognized. Still, she kept her phone ready, just in case.

By the time she reached the boathouse, the door was open and the man had gone inside. Either he'd had a key, was the world's fastest lock pick, or someone had forgotten to lock it. Any of those options were likely, and Holly made sure to make as little noise as possible as she slipped inside.

It didn't take her long to find the man wandering around a bunch of boxes that were lined up along the left wall. He had a clipboard in hand. He kept glancing at the clipboard, then at the various boxes. He looked very much like he knew what he was doing and like he belonged there, but even up close, Holly still didn't recognize him.

Finally, she stepped forward and stood just a few feet away, arms crossed in front of her chest. Doing her best to look intimidating, she glared at the man. "Can I help you with something?" she asked. Her voice was firm and demanding.

The man jumped and whirled around to face her. His eyes were wide, darting from side to side for a moment. Then, he seemed to regain his composure a bit. He smiled broadly at her, but Holly could tell it was forced. His dark brown eyes were fixated on her, and Holly could see the panic in them.

"You must be Holly," he said in an equally fake voice. He might've been able to fool other people, but Holly saw right through his false calm. "I can't believe this is the first time I've met you. I'm Dean. Randy's business partner?"

Holly narrowed her eyes. She didn't think he was lying, and she vaguely remembered Randy telling her his partner's name was

Dean, but with how he was acting, she wasn't quite sure what to believe.

"We had some of the stuff for the marina delivered here. It was easier to store it at the Inn until we needed it, you know? I'm guessing Randy didn't tell you?"

Holly shook her head. He hadn't even hinted at anything like that. For all he'd let on, he had completely cut ties with the Inn and the family. If Dad had been alive, she could've seen him asking to borrow some storage space in the boathouse. It wasn't like things were packed tight in there. It only had enough room for two boats, but it did have a lot of space for storage as well.

But she couldn't see Randy asking their mother for that privilege. Especially not after the way he had spoken on the phone last night.

Dean rolled his eyes and shook his head. "Somehow, I'm not surprised. He'd have probably called and let you know if he had shown up for work today. He probably didn't even remember I was supposed to come pick it up."

"He didn't come to work?" Holly asked, her brow rising in surprise. He had seemed fine on the phone last night, so why wouldn't he have shown up for work today?

"Nope. It's not the first time either. Knowing him, he's probably on another one of his wicked benders," Dean said with a shrug. "It's becoming more and more frequent these days. No idea what's gotten into him. But hey, now that you're here, maybe you can get through to him since I can't."

Holly blinked and nodded, lost in thought. She had known for a while Randy had a bit of a drinking problem, but she'd never known it was that bad. From the way Dean spoke, Randy was frequently missing work because of his drinking. If that was true, then he had a serious problem, and someone needed to intervene.

And yet, Holly wasn't sure she had any right to. Yes, she was the oldest. Yes, it was her job to try and look after her siblings. But it had been years since she had even attempted to be there for them. What right did she have to come and swoop in now, after all these years?

Besides, Randy was a grown man. He wasn't the dorky little kid he had been years ago when it really had been Holly's responsibility to keep him out of trouble. If she tried to confront him about his drinking and mother him, then he was likely to just buck against her and fight any help she offered.

But what else could she do? If his problem was that bad, she couldn't just sit by and let him run his life into the ground. Drinking wasn't going to make whatever problems he was going through any better. It was just going to make things worse.

Especially if he kept missing work, how long could Dean run the business with an unreliable partner? How long would it be before the business either went under or Dean decided partnering with Randy just wasn't going to work anymore?

Holly stood to the side as Dean loaded a handful of boxes onto his boat. She was so lost in thought she hadn't even asked him what they had stored in the boathouse. And by the time she did think to ask, he was waving goodbye to her and was already long gone.

Confused, Holly stood out in front of the boathouse, arms crossed in front of her chest. As if she hadn't already had enough on her plate to deal with, now she had a hundred other questions rushing through her mind.

Life in the Keys used to be simple, she thought bitterly. It was

Miami that had been fast-paced and complicated. So why was it, now that she had finally gone back to her childhood home, that it seemed like she was more lost here than she had ever been in Miami?

She needed to talk to Randy. That much was obvious. There were too many questions that only he could really answer for her. But, after the fiasco of a call they'd had last night, she was hesitant to reach out to him again.

Maybe it was better to wait a couple of days, give him some time to cool off. For all she knew, if he really had gone on a bender last night, she'd been the source of it, drudging up old memories he had been trying to keep buried.

Besides, she had enough on her plate right at that moment, and her little brother would just have to get in line.

CHAPTER SEVENTEEN

Holly stared at the half-empty glass of wine. Even after going back to the office and looking over the books again, she still hadn't been able to make heads or tails of any of it. The doctor had called to discharge her mother, and Holly had gone and picked her up.

He had given Holly a stern lecture about making sure her mother kept eating and drinking before she'd been able to leave. Her mother was awake and lucid, but it was obvious just how weak she still was. As much as Holly wanted to start questioning her about the Inn's finances and Randy's use of the boathouse, she bit her tongue.

Nelly needed to rest. Once she had recovered a bit more, they could sit down and go over everything together. Until then, Holly would just have to be patient and wait. The Inn had gotten by this far; it wasn't going to suddenly implode just because Holly waited a couple of days to untangle that particular knot.

Her phone rang, startling her enough she almost dropped her glass. Taking a deep breath, she set the glass on the table, and then fished out the phone. She frowned when she saw the name on the screen. It was almost ten o'clock at night. Why in the world was Jake calling her that late?

"Hello?" Holly answered cautiously. After how things had gone the last time she had seen Jake, she wasn't too eager to talk to him again. It was going to take a while before she truly lived down the embarrassment.

"Hey, Holly. You got a minute?" Jake asked.

For you, always, Holly thought, but she bit her tongue to keep those words from coming out of her mouth. "Yeah, I'm just sitting around thinking. Why what's up?"

Jake let out a sigh, and Holly knew immediately this wasn't about to be a social call. "I'm on nightshift tonight. And, well... There's someone here you need to come get." He tried to be as gentle as possible, but Holly's heart rate skyrocketed almost instantly.

He didn't need to clarify for Holly to know he was talking about her brother. It was the only person Jake would be calling her for.

"I'll be there as quickly as I can," she said before hanging up and stuffing the phone into her pocket. She glanced at the half-empty glass of wine, and then let out a sigh. Something told her she was going to need more than just that by the time the night was over.

She stopped by her mom's room first, checking to make sure she was doing okay. Nelly was sound asleep, though, and Holly decided not to wake her. There wasn't anything she could do but

122

worry, and there would be plenty of time for that when Holly got back.

First, she had to go pick up her younger brother and figure out what kind of trouble he had gotten himself into this time. Knowing it had been Jake who had called gave her hope that he hadn't stepped in it too badly.

She made the drive to the police station in record time. Not that it was terribly far away, since the island wasn't massive. Holly was just thankful she hadn't gotten pulled over for speeding. Because wouldn't that be just like her life? Get pulled over by a cop on the way to the police station?

When she got there, Jake was sitting at the front desk. The island's police station and police force weren't massive, but she was surprised to find him there alone. Part of her wanted to rush over and demand to see her brother; those sisterly instincts had kicked in after so many years dormant.

Instead, she forced herself to stay calm as she walked over to the man who had once stolen her heart. "Long time no see," she teased.

Jake laughed and his eyes lit up. "You know, it's been a long time since I've seen you or your siblings and now I've had two of you in my car in the same week. I'm hoping Amy and Rina aren't planning on catching a ride anytime soon."

"At least I got to sit in the front seat?" I offered with a slight smirk. She didn't have to be a mind reader to know Randy's ride hadn't been nearly as pleasant.

"You've got that right. Your brother's just lucky it was me who nabbed him and not one of the other cops. They'd have locked him up and thrown away the key." Jake sighed and shook his head. He gave Holly a sympathetic look. "He was drunk off his ass, driving down the highway toward Islamorada, like he was heading home."

Holly bit back a string of curses. It sounded like what Dean had told her really was true. Part of her hadn't wanted to believe it, but she didn't doubt Jake for even a moment. The idiot was lucky he hadn't killed anyone with a stunt like that.

Any other cop really would've locked him up without a second thought. It was a miracle Jake hadn't decided to do just that. Not yet, anyway.

"Look, I know you've all been through a lot over the last couple of years. He didn't hurt anyone, but this is going to be his only freebie. If you don't get him to straighten out, I can't make any promises next time."

"Thank you," Holly said, fighting against the emotions whirling around inside her. The look Jake gave her told Holly he hadn't done this for Randy's sake. He had done it for her. Just like when they were younger, Jake was still looking out for her. She was going to owe him big time for this.

When she looked into his eyes again, something inside her snapped. She couldn't keep it all buried inside her anymore. After everything Jake had done for her, she couldn't keep lying to him.

"You were right," she said suddenly. Jake's brow furrowed, and Holly continued. "Will and I are divorced. I'm sorry for lying to you, for not telling you right away. But it's just been the life from hell lately, and I just wasn't sure how to tell anyone."

Jake offered her a sympathetic smile, then reached out and put his hand on her shoulder. That simple gesture of reassurance was just what Holly needed to keep herself together. "I guess this is what adulthood is all about, huh?" Jake said with a smirk. When she looked into his eyes, though, Holly knew he understood exactly how she felt.

She returned his smirk as her heart skipped a beat. Holly had the urge to lean into Jake, to want his arms wrapped around her again, just like when they were young. Holly held her breath and fought against those urges, refusing to give in.

With everything going on, a relationship was not something she needed right then. Right then, she needed to find her brother and slap some sense into him. Whatever issues he was dealing with, she was going to have to help him find a new way to cope.

Thankfully, Jake must have had the same thought. He took a step back, and then nodded toward one of the doors. "Come on. He's back here in the drunk tank, no doubt trying to sleep off some of the alcohol. He's gonna have one hell of a hangover in the morning."

Jake wasn't kidding either. When he opened one of the cell doors, there was her younger brother, curled up on a metal bench, snoring away. For a long moment, Holly just stood there, hands-on-hips, staring at him and wondering how she was going to deal with him.

She glanced over at Jake and he gave her that sympathetic smile again. She wasn't sure how she would ever be able to repay him for this. If Randy thought he had issues now, she could just imagine how his life would be if he had a DUI on his record. If that had happened, a few missed days of work would've been the least of his issues.

"If I can ever repay you for this, just let me know," Holly told Jake, knowing she was going to have to do something for him. Right then, she just wasn't sure what. But the smirk Jake gave made her shiver, and she wondered just what she might've gotten herself into.

"Oh, I'm sure I can think of something." For a brief moment, Holly swore his eyes had roamed up and down her body. But considering she'd only been wearing a pair of sweatpants and an old t-shirt, she knew she had to have imagined it. Then, he turned his gaze on her sleeping brother, and she knew it had to have been just her imagination going wild. "Did you get the tire replaced on your Jag?"

Holly nodded. She took a deep breath, and then let it out slowly as she turned her own attention back to her brother. She'd had Cara drive her over to the cabana the other day, and the body shop was kind enough to meet her there with her new tire. They didn't even charge her extra for having to come out there.

But then, that was Islamadora. In Miami, she would have paid a fortune for them to even consider sending a guy out to get it. Instead, they'd have wanted her to hire a tow truck to tow it into them. Here in the Keys, though, life was different. It was slower, more intimate.

Here, they might have charged a tourist a surcharge for service like that, but even then, it wouldn't have been too much. For a local? They bent over backward to help out. Everyone did. It was the only way a place like this survived. If they didn't look out for each other, no one would be able to survive outside of the tourist season.

And even though Holly hadn't lived on the island in almost thirty years, that didn't matter to a lot of people. Once a local, always a local. At least that was their way of thinking. A lot of them thought the same way her cousin Jason did. No one ever left the islands for good. They always ended up back there, one way or another.

Holly had just taken her sweet time about it.

"I'll help you get him to the car," Jake offered. His gaze flickered between her and Randy, and Holly ran a hand through her hair as she nodded. If he was as drunk as Jake claimed, she doubted he would be able to walk on his own. And she may have been the oldest sibling, but Randy had about seven inches on her with muscle to boot.

He may have been an alcoholic, but somehow he had managed to maintain the athletic physique he'd had in school. Either working at the marina was more physically strenuous than she thought, or he was still working out regularly.

Maybe that was what he needed, Holly thought suddenly. If he wasn't working out still, getting him back to the gym might give him something to focus on other than drinking. He had started working out in middle school so he could join the football team with Dean and Logan, his best friends.

When she had visited during her college years when Randy had been in high school, it had been the same thing. His free time had always been spent in the gym or on the football field. He had still gotten into his fair share of trouble, thanks to the influence of a dozen hormonal teenagers on his team, but football had helped keep him pretty well-grounded.

She made a mental note to get ahold of Dean. He had been Randy's friend for as far back as she could remember. And since the two of them ran their business together, he was probably the one person who knew Randy best. That was going to be the best place for her to start if she really wanted to get him back on the straight and narrow.

For now, though, Holly stood in the entryway to the large cell they used as a drunk tank. They could have easily fit two dozen people in there if they'd needed to, but right then, Randy was the only resident. Come the weekend, though; there would probably be at least a half dozen, if not more, tourists sleeping off their booze.

"He better not puke in my car," Holly muttered, making Jake laugh.

"Well, if he does, let me know. I've got a buddy who does detailing, and I'm sure he would love to get his hands on that Jag of yours, even if it did mean cleaning up puke."

Holly rolled her eyes but smiled nonetheless. She would keep that in mind, but she was hoping it wouldn't come to that. But then, with the way her life seemed to be going, it was better to be prepared for anything, just in case.

She wouldn't put it passed the universe to add a ruined interior to her never-ending list of problems.

"First, we have to wake him up." Holly pursed her lips. He had to weigh at least two hundred pounds. Two hundred pounds of limp weight was not going to be easy to move, even for the two of them. If he was awake, even if he was drunk as a skunk, it would be easier to hold him up and guide him toward the car.

Holly strode forward and poked her brother in the side. He was so out of it; he didn't even move. So Holly poked him again, harder. Still no response. After a couple more jabs to his ribs still didn't rouse her drunken brother, her patience wore off.

She started swatting at him, venting out some of the frustration that had been building up inside her. At first, the lug head still didn't move, but as Holly continued to slap at her brother, he eventually started to rouse.

"Wake up, you damn idiot!" Holly yelled at her brother. "I swear to God, if I have to call Amy because of this, I'm not going to save you from her wrath!"

Out of all his sisters, Amy was the one Randy was closest to—which made sense since they were twins. Even they didn't stay in contact anymore, as far as Holly knew, but she was pretty sure Randy still wouldn't want to be on her bad side. She was the one woman in the house Randy hadn't wanted to disappoint.

"Holly?" he asked groggily. He blinked at her, but even after a few moments of staring right at her, Holly could tell he could barely see her. God, he really was drunker than she had ever seen him. "What are you doing here? Where am I?"

His words were slow and slurred as he spoke. Christ, if he was like this after having slept a bit in the cell, Holly could only imagine what he'd been like on the road. It was no wonder Jake had pulled him over, and it was a good thing he had. Randy was very lucky he hadn't hurt anyone before getting stopped.

"You're drunk, you idiot. Apparently, you decided to get wasted and tried to drive home! God, I can't believe you would do something so stupid!" Maybe she should have been a bit kinder, more understanding, but she was just too annoyed right then to be a doting motherly figure to the man. Besides, he probably wouldn't even remember this come morning. "Now get your butt up so we can get you in my car. And, I swear to God Randall Alvin Archer, if you puke in my car, they will never find your body!"

Jake chuckled from behind Holly. The sound must've caught Randy's attention, since he tried, and failed, to look at its source.

"You know, as a cop, I really should say something about those threats, but I think this time I'm just gonna pretend I didn't hear anything."

"Smart idea," Holly said dryly, though she couldn't quite hold back her smirk. "Now help me haul my lug head brother outside and stuff him into the passenger seat of the Jag."

CHAPTER EIGHTEEN

HOLLY SIPPED AT HER STEAMING COFFEE. SHE WANTED MORE than anything to just chug the entire mug in the hopes it might make her headache go away, but she knew if she did that, she would just end up burning her mouth and throat.

"It looks like I'm not the only one who needs some bed rest," Nelly teased. She sat on the opposite side of the kitchen table, a mug of coffee set in front of her alongside the eggs and bacon Holly had cooked up for breakfast.

She still looked quite weak and frail, but there was more life in her eyes than Holly had seen since she had returned to the Keys. The depression meds really seemed to be helping with her mother's energy levels, which in turn was helping with everything else.

As long as she kept on this path, Holly was becoming more confident her mother really would make a full recovery. It would no doubt take time, but that was the one thing they seemed to have in abundance right then.

A thudding sound on the stairs caught both their attention. Holly winced as her mother turned in the direction of the stairs, worry evident in her eyes. Last night, she had barely managed to get Randy up to his old bedroom before she had gone to her room to collapse.

And so far this morning, she hadn't had the chance to tell their mother about what had happened last night. So when Randy appeared in the doorway, looking very much like he'd been run over by a truck last night, Nelly squealed in surprise.

The woman moved faster than she should've been able to in her condition. She rushed over to wrap her arms around her only son. Randy stared in surprise for a moment, and then carefully hugged her back.

"Oh, my God!" Nelly squealed loud enough they could probably hear her back at the Inn. "I can't believe you're here! Oh, Randy! It's been so long since I've seen you. And I swear you've somehow managed to grow since then!"

Randy forced out a laugh. He locked eyes with Holly for a moment as if trying to reassure himself that this wasn't a dream. "Still the same height, Mom," he said carefully. "Haven't grown an inch since I was eighteen."

"Then, I must be shrinking!" Nelly declared. Finally, she pried herself away from her son just long enough to take his hand and guide him over to the table. Even though she was supposed to be the one resting and being taken care of, she busied herself getting Randy a cup of coffee and a plate of food before Holly could even say anything.

Randy had a look of shock on his face like he wasn't sure this was all really happening. Holly couldn't blame him. He probably didn't remember a single thing from the previous night. All he knew was he'd randomly woken up in his childhood bed. And now, the woman he had been so sure had hated him, was doting on him like he was her favorite child.

It really must have been like he was in a dream.

Holly smirked as she sipped at her coffee and watched the scene in front of her. Nelly didn't once ask why Randy was there or when he'd gotten there. No doubt, she had taken one look at him and decided she didn't want to know, which was just fine with Holly.

Nelly didn't need that stress right now. Once they were alone, Holly would talk to her brother, try and get him back on the right path. If she could do that, then Nelly would never need to know about his monumental mistake.

Once she finished her coffee, Holly left the two of them to catch up while she went to do the rounds and check up on the staff. Most of them had been working at the Inn for ages, so they knew how to do their jobs without her having to hover over their shoulders. But she still liked to check in regularly and make sure no new crisis had popped up.

By the time she returned to the Archer House, Randy was sitting out on the porch on one of the small swings that had always sat there overlooking the water. He looked a bit more put together than he had that morning, but his eyes were still bloodshot and he looked more than a little lost.

Holly stood on the stairs leading up the porch and the two of them locked eyes. Randy at least looked sheepish, knowing Holly had bailed him out the night before. She could also see gratitude in his gaze. Whether it was from her helping him out or from her not spilling everything to their mother, she wasn't sure.

Not that it really mattered. When it came to things they needed to talk about, that was probably near the bottom.

She nodded toward the pier, not far from the house. A single boat was tethered there, bobbing up and down on the gentle waves. "I checked out Dad's boat the other day. It's still in pretty good shape. Why don't we get out on the water for a bit?"

Randy frowned but nodded. When he stood from the bench, Holly noticed how slowly he moved. No doubt, he was still nursing that hangover and would be for at least the day. But hey, a hangover was probably the easiest of the potential consequences.

Their dad's old boat wasn't anything special. A twenty-four-foot center console he had bought used and restored himself. It had just barely fit the six of them, though as they'd gotten older, rarely did all of them ever go out at the same time.

Right then, it would be perfect for the two of them to get away from everything and just talk.

Randy took control of the moment they stepped on board. And, in minutes, they were out on the crystal blue ocean, the shore getting farther and farther away with each passing moment. Neither of them spoke until the beach was only barely visible in the distance.

"You're an idiot; you know that?" Holly told him. She wasn't angry this time, but she wasn't going to lie to him either. What he had done last night was beyond stupid, and he needed to understand that.

Randy winced, but he nodded. Chewing on his bottom lip, he

stared out over the water. "I'm guessing by the fact my truck isn't here that I didn't drive here on my own."

Holly snorted and shook her head. Just as she thought, he didn't remember any of the previous night. "Not even close, though you were apparently on your way down here when Jake pulled you over, drunk as a skunk."

Again, Randy winced. He didn't even look over at Holly. He may have been prone to making stupid mistakes, but he wasn't dumb. He knew what he had done last night was irresponsible and foolish. And he knew what the potential consequences could have been.

"You're right, I am an idiot," he said at last.

Holly sighed, and then went to sit next to him. He had been lucky. No one had gotten hurt, and it had been Jake who had caught him. That meant this wasn't a life-ending mistake. It was one he could learn from, provided he never made it again.

"What's going on, Randy?" Holly asked in a gentle voice. It had been a long time since she had taken up this role for her siblings, but she slipped back into it with ease. "Talk to me."

"I just— I panicked. When you called and told me about Mom being sick. I freaked out. I didn't know what to do. So I went to the bar to have a drink to help calm my nerves. And one drink turned into two and then three and then..."

He didn't have to continue for Holly to understand. Addiction wasn't something you could just turn on or off. Once he had gotten started, he couldn't stop himself.

"God, I swear I'm always the family fuck-up. It doesn't matter how old I get. I'm constantly messing everything up." Randy still stared out at the water. His entire body was tense and stiff. More than anything, Holly wanted to pull him into her arms and tell him it would all be okay. But while they were making progress in their relationship, they weren't quite to that point yet. "It always seemed like no one other than Dad ever had time for me. And I mean, why would they? You've always had your life together. Even Amy and Rina were always doing better than me."

Holly let out a snort. That caused Randy to look over at her; finally, his eyes narrowed. She smirked and shook her head. "Christ, it only looks like I have my life together. In fact..." Holly took a deep breath and held it. There wasn't going to be any better time than this, but it still wasn't easy. "Will and I got divorced. He got involved in some shady business deals and ruined our entire business. All I've got left is the bit of money I squirreled away."

Randy looked at her like she had two heads and finally said, "That's why you jumped at the chance to come back."

"What other choice did I have? There wasn't anything left for me back in Miami. At least here... here I feel like there's something I can be doing, you know? Like I have some kind of purpose, at least for a little while."

Randy nodded. He looked at his eldest sister for a while, and Holly wondered what he was thinking. Finally, he reached out and put a hand on her knee. "I guess there's a lot I was wrong about. Like how Mom felt about me. Your life. God only knows what else."

"There's still plenty of time to fix all of that," Holly nudged her brother gently. "Why don't you stick around for a while? Your girls are with their mother, and it's not that far of a commute to the marina. You don't have to help out around the Inn, but I'm sure Mom would love having you around for a little while."

"Maybe I will..." Randy let out a sigh and gave her the barest smile.

She wasn't going to be able to fix all of his problems at once. Certainly not in a single conversation! But they had made some good progress, and really, that was all she had hoped for from this little jaunt out on the water.

Just like Nelly, Randy was back on the right track. It was going to be a long journey and it wasn't going to be easy, but if he worked at it, he could get his life back together.

And just maybe, so could Holly.

She thought about asking him about Dean and why he was loading boxes onto his boat the other day, then decided against it. Things were good between them right now. And after everything else they both had to deal with, it just didn't seem all that important.

There would be time to deal with all of that later. And now that Randy was around, he could help take some of the stress off her shoulders. She could focus on making sure the Inn didn't fall apart, and he could help make sure their mother didn't slip back into depression.

Maybe together, they could salvage the Inn.

CHAPTER NINETEEN

"I TOLD YOU; YOU DON'T HAVE TO HELP WITH THIS," HOLLY said as Randy started unloading supplies from the back of his truck. She had taken him back to his place a few days ago, and then he'd driven back with some clothes and other things he wanted while he stayed there.

And when Holly had discussed wanting to spruce up a few cabins that sat along the beach, which were only a short walk from the main Inn, Randy had jumped at the chance to help. She wasn't sure what had gotten into him but figured he had his own reasons and she didn't want to pry.

"Gotta keep myself busy," he said with a smirk, hoisting a ladder from the back of the truck as if it were made from paper. Holly let out a low whistle, and Randy's grin broadened. Clearly, he really hadn't let himself go at all! There must've been something in the water around this place. "Besides, you may be Miss Perfect, but something tells me you don't work with your hands very often."

Heat rushed to her cheeks as she pursed her lips. Ever since their chat on the boat, Randy liked to teasingly call her Miss Perfect. That alone didn't bother her, but he was right about her not having spent much time working with her hands.

She knew all about how to fix up a house. You couldn't be a real estate agent and not know what work a place needed to be able to sell for top dollar. And sure, when she had first gotten started, she had done some of the work herself to save a bit of money. But it had been years since then. More recently, she had crews she worked with that could handle anything and everything a house needed to be put on the market at top dollar.

But it was just like riding a bike, wasn't it? She was certain she could handle the basics of sprucing the cabins up. It wasn't like she was going to completely remodel them. She just wanted to get the easy stuff out of the way, so Jason and Paul's crews didn't have to deal with minor stuff.

With the Inn's finances still in flux, she could only afford to pay them for so much. And if that meant she had to get out there on a ladder with a paintbrush or a screwdriver, then that was what she was going to do.

Though truth be told, she did appreciate Randy's help. She just didn't appreciate him teasing her about it.

"Aww, don't pout at me," Randy teased, winking at her. It was strange, the two of them joking around like they were kids again, but Holly kind of liked it. It was a new start for the two of them. "You said this one's empty for two days, right? Then I'll get the ladder set up and work on the exterior, and you can head inside and start touching up the paint in there. How's that sound?"

It certainly sounded faster than doing it all herself, that was for sure!

So she took one of the smaller buckets of paint and a couple of different sized brushes and used her master key to unlock the cabin. The interior didn't look all that bad. It was clean, at the very least, but there were a good number of places where the paint was faded or chipped just from years of wear and tear.

Nothing some good old fashioned elbow grease wouldn't fix though!

She had purposely worn an old pair of jeans and a t-shirt she had pilfered from her brother, just so she wouldn't have to worry about getting paint all over herself. With her hair tied up in a tight bun, she was ready to get to business and breathe some fresh life into the cabin.

Holly wasn't sure how long it took before she had finally finished touching up each of the rooms, but she was dripping with sweat by the end of it. And that had been inside with the AC running! She could only imagine how her brother was faring outside in the sun!

Gathering up her supplies again, she headed back outside. Randy was around the back of the cabin now, and while Holly was sweating, he was drenched. At some point, he had taken off his t-shirt and draped it against one of the window sills to dry, leaving him shirtless in the sunlight.

If Randy was looking to find himself a new woman, all he had to do was keep working around the Inn like that! Holly thought with a laugh. She doubted very many of the women on the island, locals or otherwise, would turn down a well-muscled man who was good with his hands!

Randy must've noticed her watching him. He shouted down to her, a teasing lilt in his voice. "See something you like, sis?"

Holly rolled her eyes. She wasn't even going to go there. Instead, she just returned his smirk. "Just wondering if that life insurance policy Mom had taken out on all of us was still valid. I'm pretty sure falling off a ladder was one of the covered provisions."

Randy's laughter echoed around them. He finished the last spot he was working on, and then headed down the ladder to join her on solid ground once more. "Just remember, Mom had one of those policies on you, too. And after going through the divorce with Patty, I've had lots of time to consider various ways to make a death seem accidental!"

"Oh please," Holly waved off his comments with a flip of her hand. "We all know you would never harm the hair on a woman, Randall Archer. I'm pretty sure Dad more than drilled that into you growing up!"

Randy pouted. With his brow scrunched up and lips pursed, he suddenly wasn't a forty-two-year-old man anymore. He was the bratty eight-year-old who would always complain if he got left out of anything the girls were doing. "Yeah, that was totally not fair. You three could wail on me all you wanted and he wouldn't say a word. But if I dared get you back for any of it? He tanned my hide from one end of the island to the other!"

"And here you thought *you* were Dad's favorite. You may have been his only son, but there's nothing quite like the bond between a father and daughter!" Holly reached out and playfully shoved her brother. When he shoved her right back, she stared at him, mouth hanging open.

"It's a good thing Dad's not around to spank me then!" Randy's laughter filled the air, and Holly had the sudden urge to dunk her brother in the ocean like she had done so many times growing up. She had done it to all three of her siblings actually— more times than she could count.

"Well, if you don't mind putting your childhood revenge on hold, we've got one more cabin to work on today. Number three checked out this morning and the new guests won't be here until late tomorrow night, so we've got just enough time to get it looking good for them."

Randy let out a dramatic sigh as he shook his head. "And here I thought I had come back home for some rest and relaxation. Now I've got my big sister cracking the whip again. What did I get myself into?"

"Keep it up and I'll really crack the whip!" Holly threatened.

The two of them took their time loading everything back into Randy's truck. Then they each grabbed a bottle of water from the cooler back there and chugged it down. While Holly didn't want to dawdle, she also didn't want either of them collapsing from heatstroke or something.

Besides, it wasn't like the touch-ups needed to be done right that very second. From what Natalie had told her, the new guests weren't due to arrive until at least eight in the evening. That gave them plenty of time to work on it today, then have it dry and aired out for the guests by tomorrow.

When they finally did make it over to Cabin Three, they divvied up the duties the same way again. Holly had offered to take the outdoor work this time, but Randy wouldn't hear anything of it. Despite his earlier teasing, he was still too much of a gentleman to let his sister be the one melting in the Florida sun.

Cabin three didn't need nearly as much paint touch-ups as cabin one had. Instead, Holly found herself going through the place and tightening various cabinets and doors, oiling the ones that were squeaking. The cabin, and the others, would need new carpet laid and some other work done, but that would have to be handled by one of her cousins or someone on their crew.

She had just stepped outside for some fresh air and another bottle of water when she heard someone shouting. Walking around to the side of the cabin, she found Randy halfway up his ladder, brush in hand.

"You yell for me?" Holly asked before taking another long gulp of water.

Randy shook his head. "Nope. Was just about to come down and see if it was you yelling for me."

"Probably one of the guests yelling for their kids or their dog or something," Holly said with a shrug. While the entire grounds were pretty calm and relaxing, this was still a prime vacation spot for families. That meant there was a certain amount of noise that was around all day long.

But when the voice yelled again, Holly was pretty sure it was someone calling her name. The furrowed look Randy gave her said he had heard the same thing. She stepped aside as he made his way down the ladder, then the two of them headed back around the cabin, searching for the source of the noise.

Holly could just make out a figure wandering around when the person yelled again. This time, Holly was positive they were calling her name. Part of her wanted to call out in response, but she had no idea who it was calling for her. For all she knew, it was some ax murderer coming to make her his next victim.

But when the figure got closer, Holly realized it wasn't an ax murderer. Well, she wasn't one yet. But after Holly had ignored her calls and forgotten to call her back, she wouldn't have put it passed her daughter to be out for blood.

"Gabby!" Holly yelled in her daughter's direction. "What in the world are you doing out here?"

"The woman at the desk told me you would be out by the cabins," Gabby yelled back. And even at a distance, Holly could hear more than just irritation in her daughter's voice.

No doubt it had been Natalie who had told her where Holly was hiding out. But that wasn't the issue. The issue was what Gabby was doing in the Keys in the first place. She should have still been back in Miami, not all the way down here.

When Gabby approached, Holly smiled and went to hug her daughter. But the glare Gabby gave her stopped her midway. Gabby was most definitely not happy. Whatever had brought her all the way down here was not going to be good news.

"Mom, I swear to God! I have to drive for hours just to talk to you now?" Gabby said. The anger was evident just below the surface. "I thought you would be back in Miami by now, but apparently not. You had us both scared to death! What's going on that's so important you can't even pick up the phone when your own daughter calls?"

Holly flinched, her daughter's accusations stabbing her right in the heart. She should have called Gabby back that night, instead of putting it off. Instead, she'd let herself get caught up in everything else going on and had completely forgotten about it.

Just because Gabby wasn't a child anymore didn't mean she didn't need her mother. Holly wasn't the only one who'd had their life completely turned upside down when Will's schemes had gone public. It had affected both of their children as well, even though they were adults with their own lives.

No doubt, it had led to a lot of uncertainty and confusion on their part. As far as they'd known, Holly and Will were perfectly happy in their marriage. They were the epitome of a happy, successful couple and to Gabby and Sean, watching that all come crumbling down had probably shaken them to their core.

If their parents' perfect marriage could fall apart, what did that mean for their own relationships?

God, Holly should have seen all of that ages ago. She should have sat both kids down and talked to them, explained everything. She should've been there for them, let them express their fears and concerns so Holly could put them at ease.

And yet, the first chance she had gotten to run away from Miami and not look back, she had taken it. She hadn't told the kids before she had left. She hadn't even kept them up to date since arriving in the Keys.

Once again, Holly had let herself get swept away with work that she'd neglected her family. Sure, she had been there for her mother and Randy when they'd needed her, but she hadn't been there for her own two children.

Holly locked eyes with her daughter. Gabby didn't need to use words for her mother to understand everything. She may not have been Mother of the Year, but Holly still knew her daughter. She could look into those dark brown eyes and know everything Gabby was feeling.

And it wasn't because of some super special mother-daughter connection. Holly could tell what her daughter was thinking and feeling because Gabby was just like she was. If she had stopped and paid more attention, maybe she would have seen it sooner, but she and Gabby were exactly alike.

Which meant Holly had work to do. If she didn't get her butt into gear and fix the hundred and one problems she had created, Gabby might end up going down the same road she had. Holly couldn't let that happen.

Gabby had her whole life ahead of her—a fiancé who doted on her. She had a job she adored, teaching third graders. There was no way Holly could let Gabby make the same mistakes she had made.

"Come on, let's go talk," Holly said, trying to smile. When she glanced over at Randy, he raised an eyebrow. "Can you finish the cabin up? I have a feeling this is gonna take a while."

CHAPTER TWENTY

THE TWO OF THEM HEADED AWAY FROM THE FAMILY INN. Holly wanted to put some distance between it and herself for this conversation. If she stayed too close, she was afraid some minor problems might crop up and try to pull her attention away once again.

Besides, Gabby had only been to Islamorada a handful of times over the years. Since she was there, Holly figured she might as well let her daughter see some of the town where her mother had grown up.

They headed toward the Founders Park. Holly had taken Gabby there when she was a baby or a toddler, but judging by the way Gabby was trying to take it all in, she didn't remember much if any of it.

It was a gorgeous place, and one of the first sites tourists flock to when they came to town. Maybe once the summer was over and the place settled down, Holly would have her come back so they could really enjoy it together.

That thought made Holly's breath catch in her throat. She hadn't made any formal plans to stay for any certain length of time, but there she was, already thinking as if she would be around for the long haul. Once again, without discussing it with anyone.

"I'm sorry I didn't answer your calls that day. Grandma... Grandma isn't doing well. I was at the hospital with her when you had tried to call, and I just couldn't talk at the moment. But I should have called you back the moment I was able to."

Gabby nodded absently. She listened quietly as Holly filled her in on everything regarding Nelly's incident. Her daughter's anger dissipated and was replaced by concern for the grandmother she had only met a handful of times.

"I'm glad she's doing better," Gabby said, the edge in her voice gone now. Just like Holly, she didn't stay angry for very long. She had a quick fuse, but it was thankfully a short one, a fact that would probably save her from a lot of headaches in the future.

She had known too many people who didn't know when to give up, and they were almost always miserable. That was certainly not a fate she would ever want to wish on her daughter.

They walked in silence for a bit longer, Gabby taking in the sights like a tourist. But then, she was a tourist, wasn't she? Neither she nor Sean had gotten to grow up on the island, and Holly regretted not bringing them back here more often.

Eventually, the Inn would pass to Holly and her siblings. And then, after that, it would go on to Gabby, Sean, and their cousins. It didn't seem right for them not to have grown up around the Archer Inn, learning it from the ground up like she had.

Just another regret she would have to live with, Holly thought to herself.

"Mom," Gabby said suddenly, breaking the silence. "What's really going on with you and Dad? Your lawyers keep calling us and showing up at the houses trying to find you. Sean and I aren't stupid, you know. So stop lying and just tell me the truth, please."

Holly muttered curses under her breath. She had told Will to handle the IRS, but if the lawyers were still hounding for her, that meant he hadn't done it yet. If he didn't do something soon, Holly was likely to end up in prison for something she had nothing to do with.

But how was she supposed to explain that to her daughter? Wouldn't that just freak her out? Worse, wouldn't that just make her angrier with her father? But she couldn't keep lying to her and Sean forever. If the worst-case scenario really did come to pass, then she wouldn't want them to be blindsided by it.

"Your father... You know he was involved in some shady real estate deals. Well, as it turned out, he had been falsifying all of the tax records, too, trying to cover his tracks. But once the shady deals came to light, so did the stuff with his taxes..." Holly took a deep breath. Everything was good so far, but how much more should she have to tell Gabby?

Before she could decide that question, Gabby cut in. She stopped walking and grabbed Holly's wrist, forcing her mother to turn and look into her eyes. "Mom. I'm pregnant."

"Wha... what?" Holly stammered out. Her eyes went wide as her mind went into overdrive. Gabby was... pregnant? Was that what she had wanted to tell her in person when they had talked last? Her heart pounded faster and faster with each passing moment.

Tourists wandered around them, not paying them any attention. Holly didn't notice any of them, though. In her mind, it was just the two of them standing there together, as Holly tried to fully comprehend the bombshell her daughter had just dropped on her.

She was going to have another grandbaby? She had known this would probably happen at some point, but it had always seemed like some far off time. But then, it had felt like that when Sean had told her his girlfriend had been pregnant.

Though in his case, they hadn't even been engaged, so it had been a bit more of a shock. But Gabby and Lucas were set to be married within the next year. They had to be over the moon about the news.

And yet, as Holly stared into her daughter's eyes, she knew that wasn't the truth. She didn't see the excitement and joy she would expect from a mother-to-be. Instead, she just saw fear and panic. Her baby girl looked ready to burst into tears at any moment, and Holly's heart broke as she pulled Gabby into a hug.

"I don't know if I can do it," Gabby said as she fought back the tears. "I... I always thought I would be overjoyed to have a baby with Lucas. I mean, I love him to death and I can't wait to start a family, but after everything with you and Dad... I just... I don't know anymore."

Holly's chest's tightened. She had to fight just to breathe as her daughter shook against her. It was no wonder Gabby had seemed so urgent about the two of them talking in person. She was even more of a mess than Holly had thought, and Holly cursed herself once again for having let things get away from her.

"You and Dad... You guys always seemed so happy together. I never, ever, thought he could be capable of something like this. But if he was able to lie to you and keep secrets from you and then try to run off and hide instead of taking responsibility... What's to say, Lucas won't do the same thing in the future?"

Holly's heart continued to break. She opened and closed her mouth several times, trying to find the words that might ease her daughter's mind. But no matter how hard she tried, she just couldn't figure out what it was, she was supposed to say.

What had happened with Will had absolutely shattered her when she had first found out. It was only now that she was slowly beginning to put those pieces of herself back together. It was no wonder Gabby would be terrified of the same thing happening to her.

"I don't want to look back in twenty-six years and feel like my entire life was a disaster. I just... I don't know what to do, Mom. I haven't even told Lucas about the baby yet."

Holly had been right, back at the Inn. This was a train she needed to get in front of before it sped out of control, assuming she wasn't already too late to stop it. But this was her only daughter, her baby girl. She had to find some way to fix everything for her, to give her the shot at a better life than Holly had.

She squeezed her daughter tight. She may not have known exactly what she needed to say to make things right, but she would figure it out. She wasn't Superwoman or even Supermom. But dang it, she was not going to let her daughter go through this alone. One way or another, she would figure this out.

But she didn't have to do it alone, she realized. None of them had to go through all these problems by themselves. Heck, maybe that was the whole reason the universe had sent her back here, back to Islamorada after so many years.

Here, she still had family. She still had friends. Here, she had help. Just as much as Nelly and Randy needed her help, she realized she needed their help too. None of them could shoulder their burdens alone. But, together, just maybe they could all figure it out.

CHAPTER TWENTY-ONE

I<small>T TOOK A LITTLE WHILE FOR</small> G<small>ABBY TO CALM DOWN ENOUGH</small> for Holly to do anything. She stood there, in the middle of the park, and just held her daughter. If Gabby had needed her to stand there all night and hug her, then that was what Holly was going to do.

But, eventually, her tears subsided. She still shook and the look in her eyes told her the tears could return at any moment. The middle of a busy park wasn't the best place for them to try and figure this all out, Holly decided, and after a few more moments to make sure Gabby was a bit more stable, they headed out.

Holly didn't want to go back to the Inn just yet. There was too much going on there right now, and Holly wanted to be able to give Gabby her complete focus for a bit longer. Instead, she decided to take her to Mel's cabana bar. It wasn't the most private of locations, but if they could snag a table in the back, they would have enough privacy to talk without everyone in the world overhearing.

That would have to do for now.

Thankfully, it was between lunch and dinner when they had arrived, so the place wasn't very busy at all. The hostess seemed surprised they wanted a table inside rather than one of the ones out on the beach. While there were a handful of people outside enjoying a late lunch or early dinner, there was next to no one sitting inside.

Which was just perfect for them. That would give Holly and Gabby some time to talk before the crowds started showing up.

"I still can't believe this happened," Gabby said, her hands resting on her stomach. "I mean, I guess I can. It's not like we were being super careful or anything like that. We're engaged, you know? And I mean, eventually, I wanted to have kids with him. It's just... now..."

Holly nodded her understanding. Having kids in the future was one thing. Getting a sudden surprise, right in the middle of the world, being topsy-turvy was a completely different scenario. And while she had no doubt Gabby and Lucas would make amazing parents, she completely understood her daughter's fears.

"Lucas isn't like your father," Holly said, choosing her words carefully. "I've seen the way he treats you. The way he talks to you. Your father was never abusive or anything, but he never doted on me the way Lucas dotes on you."

Gabby blinked for a moment and then smiled just a bit. Her eyes clouded over, and Holly knew she was lost in a memory. Probably some romantic gesture Lucas had done for her at some point.

Now that Holly thought about it, how often had Will done

romantic things for her? Ones he had done just to surprise her or make her happy, without anyone else around to give him brownie points? Maybe it was just the lingering resentment, but try as she might, she couldn't think of a single time.

"Has Lucas ever once done anything to make you think you can't trust him? Even the smallest thing?" Holly asked. She could think of a number of things Will had done over the years. Nothing that would outright raise red flags, but all together and with the power of hindsight, there were clues all throughout their relationship.

Gabby pursed her lips as she considered the question. She thought about it for a long while, and Holly sat patiently, not wanting to rush her daughter. "No," she said at last. "He's always been an open book. I mean, I don't hover over him or anything, but he never really hides anything from me. I know the password to his phone, not that I ever check it. Same with his laptop."

"You think your father ever gave me the passwords to anything that wasn't directly related to my work at the company? Not that I ever asked for them. Back then, I hadn't ever had a reason to. But he would have never volunteered that information. If Lucas did, then that should tell you something right there."

"Yeah," Gabby said quietly as she nodded. Once again, she was lost in thought. This was all so much for her to process and come to terms with. It was going to take time for her to truly figure out how she felt about everything, instead of just letting her emotions run rampant.

But Gabby had something to look forward to. She may not have realized it just yet, but that tiny baby growing inside her would completely change her life. Babies were something special. They gave you this sense of hope and positivity that Holly had never been able to replicate in the years since she'd had hers.

Heck, just knowing she had a grandbaby on the way had sparked something inside of Holly. She had been slowly figuring things out and piecing herself back together. But now... Now she had something new and exciting to look forward to.

She remembered the time she had spent with her granddaughter Rachel as a baby, how looking into her big, beady eyes had filled her with so much joy and excitement. God, how had she let that get away from her? That right there should have been the pivotal moment in her life. But it hadn't been. She had gone right back to work, burying herself neck-deep in it.

"You can do this, Gabby. You and Lucas are going to be amazing parents. And he's going to be an amazing husband." Holly reached across the table and took her daughter's hands in hers. She squeezed them tight and locked eyes with Gabby, not breaking eye contact for even a moment. "I have more regrets about my past than I can count. But, you know what? I've got even more moments that I wouldn't trade for the world. Like you and Sean."

Gabby stared at her for a moment, and then blinked away the tears that had started to form. She nodded and smiled, a real smile, for the first time since she had arrived in the Keys.

Just like everything else, her problems weren't going to be solved in an instant. But they had time, and together they would figure it all out.

"Well, well, well," a voice said from across the restaurant. Holly looked up to see a grinning Melissa heading toward them. "First, I don't see you for years at a time, and now I've seen you three times in a week. The world really must be coming to an end."

Holly grinned and stood, hugging Mel when she walked over. "Nah, it's just finally starting to right itself out. You remember my daughter, Gabby?"

"Of course I do. And it's not like she's not the spitting image of her mother." Mel winked at her, and then gave Gabby a quick hug. "What brings you to our tiny little town? I hope you're not planning on whisking your mother back to Miami already. She just got here."

Gabby and Holly exchanged a look. That was one of the benefits of them being so much alike. They didn't always need words to communicate with each other. Gabby gave her mother a slight smile and a nod, answering her silent question.

"Well, if you must know, Gabby drove all the way down here to give me the good news. She's pregnant with her first child."

Melissa's eyes went wide. Her mouth hung open and she looked very much like the air had just been knocked from her lungs. "Oh, my God! What wonderful news," she yelled, her voice echoing across the restaurant. Holly hadn't realized just how long they had been there. Already a small group of people had trickled into the place, mostly older locals who wanted dinner before it became a zoo with tourists.

"That's gotta be the best thing I've heard all day!" Melissa pulled Gabby into another hug, squeezing her tight. Holly's best friend was bouncing up and down with excitement, making Holly laugh. "I think that calls for a little celebration. I'll be right back!"

Neither of them had a chance to inquire what Melissa had

meant by that before the woman had disappeared back into the kitchen. They looked at each other for a moment, and then both burst out laughing. They wore matching grins now and at least for a little while, all of their worries and stress had been put on the back burner.

Before Melissa could return, the early bird guests started making their way over to their table, offering their congratulations to Gabby. Gabby stood there, wide-eyed, as Holly introduced the various people to her. Most of them Holly hadn't seen in decades, but they all seemed to remember as if it was only yesterday.

"Don't even ask me how old she is," Holly whispered to her daughter as an elderly woman was escorted back to her table. "Misses Thompson was ancient when she was my first-grade teacher. I'm pretty sure she's secretly a witch and found a spell for immortality."

Gabby put her hands over her mouth to stifle her laughter. By the time Melissa returned with two of the largest desserts Holly had ever laid eyes on, Gabby had looked positively overwhelmed. Having lived her whole life in Miami, she had never gotten to experience the charm of a small town where everyone knew everyone and where gossip spread like wildfire.

Heck, there was a good chance the rest of the family would know about Gabby's news by the time they got back to the Inn. But that was a risk you took when you lived in the Keys, and even though Gabby was overwhelmed, she had a broad grin on her face as she dug into the cookie-brownie-sundae concoction Melissa and her chef had created just for them.

"I'm starting to think it's not the baby that makes you fat when you're pregnant but the cravings!"

Holly laughed and grinned just as broadly. "Oh, honey. Let me tell you; the cravings are just the beginning. Before you know it, you'll be wanting to eat non-stop!"

"Well, then maybe I should stick around, at least for a little while. I can't think of anywhere in Miami that makes food like this place!" Gabby looked around the little restaurant appreciatively. It wasn't much to look at, at least not the little inside portion, but Gabby wasn't wrong. There wasn't anywhere in Miami that quite had this place's charm or delicious cooking.

"You'd be welcome to stay as long as you would like." Holly didn't even bother asking her mother. Gabby was an Archer. Even after she got married, she would still be an Archer. And Archers were always welcomed at the Archer House and the Inn.

Family didn't turn away family, not ever.

"Your grandmother's going to be so surprised when she finds out the news, though. If you think Melissa got excited, just wait until you get back to the house!" Holly could already see her mother jumping up and down for joy. She had been out of this world when Sean had had his baby three years ago. She was going to be just as excited about this one.

Yes, this was what the universe had been guiding her towards. And not just her either but the entire family. This baby would give all of them a fresh breath of life again. It was just what Nelly needed to keep pushing forward, and it would remind Randy there were still good things in life to look forward to.

And as for Holly? She couldn't even express just how she felt knowing she had another grandbaby on the way. Even when life seemed like it was nothing but doom and gloom, there was always a dawn if you just waited and looked for it.

It wasn't there just yet, but Holly felt herself inching closer and closer to it. And yet, at the same time, she was also apprehensive, like she was waiting for the other shoe to drop. But she refused to focus on those feelings and kept them locked up and buried away.

She wasn't about to let her anxiety ruin a good thing!

CHAPTER TWENTY-TWO

Just as Holly had expected, her mother was over the moon with the news. Even Randy was in a better mood, and dinner that night was practically a feast. Nelly ate more in that one meal than Holly had seen her eat since she had gotten there, so that had to be a good sign.

In fact, over the next few days, she was positively upbeat. That alone gave Holly hope for the future. Gabby also insisted on helping Holly and Randy with the maintenance around the Inn. Holly had suggested she rest instead, being pregnant and all, but a single look from her daughter put an end to that.

It was a couple of days after Gabby had gotten there. They were all sitting around the dining room table, having just finished dinner. Gabby had been quiet for most of the meal, and when Holly asked if she was okay, she gave her mother a strange look.

"You said the Archer Inn has been a staple of the island for decades, right?" Gabby asked. Everyone else at the table exchanged looks and then nodded. "Well, then it makes sense the island would want to see it restored to its former glory, right? So why don't we set up a fundraiser or something? I'm sure at least a couple of the people would be willing to pitch in, from what I've seen."

No one said anything for a few moments. Holly's mind raced with idea after idea, each building on the next. Gabby was right. The locals all looked out for each other for the most part. No doubt, they would be disappointed at the current state of the Inn. Maybe enough to pitch in to help bring it back to life.

All of a sudden, everyone was speaking at once. Nelly went off to get some notepads and pens from the office, and then they all went to work planning the entire thing out. It wouldn't be cheap to do it right, but from what Holly had read in the books, they had enough cash on hand for it. And, if it was successful, they would bring in much more than they would spend.

Once the plans were laid out, everyone had their role. Even Nelly was going to be put to work for this one, though her job was easily done from the couch or from the bed if she wanted. She had the task of inviting everyone she could to come to the event since Holly was pretty sure Nelly knew every single local on the island.

It took a couple more days to bring their ideas to fruition, but on a sunny Saturday morning, everything was ready to go.

And boy had Gabby been right about the islanders wanting to help out. From what Holly could tell, every single resident of Islamorada was in attendance, and the grounds of the Inn were positively packed with people from the main grounds to the beach area where they had their volleyball nets set up.

At fifty dollars a head, Holly struggled to calculate just how much money they had brought in.

Holly and her family mingled with the crowd of people, shaking hands and thanking everyone for coming to help out. Nelly and Randy went off on their own; seeking out the people they knew best while Gabby stuck close to her mother.

Holly could barely contain her laughter as almost every person she introduced Gabby to inquired about the baby. Gabby seemed shocked each time someone asked since she didn't know any of these people. But on Islamorada, that didn't matter. They all knew her, whether she liked it or not.

That was the beauty of a small town!

"What, are you trying to put me out of work?" A deep voice called from behind her. Holly whirled around to see Jake standing there, dressed in his uniform, grinning. "Guess there's not gonna be much crime today if every danged person on the island is here!"

"Well, you know me. I just wanted to do my part to keep our island safe," Holly teased. She winked at him, and then slid an arm around Gabby's waist. "Jake Holton, meet my daughter Gabrielle."

"Gabby, please," she said as she extended a hand.

"It's a pleasure to meet you. Has anyone ever told you you're the spitting image of your mother?"

Gabby giggled and nodded. "I've heard that quite a bit today. I mean, I've seen the pictures of Mom from when she was younger, but it's one thing to look at those and another to hear everyone she grew up with telling me how I look just like her."

"Well, let's hope for her sake you're not as wild and crazy as she was growing up!"

"Wild and crazy, huh?" Gabby's eyes went wide for a moment. Then, she turned to her mother and grinned. "Are you sure he's talking about you? Because I'm not sure, I can believe that you were ever wild and crazy."

Holly shot Jake a mock glare. "Well, I had my moments. But I think we can spare everyone a trip down memory lane. Wouldn't want to give my daughter the wrong impression, would we?"

"I think you mean you don't want me giving her any ideas. Like that time after Sam Holland's party during our senior year..."

"Jacob Holton!" Holly warned, cutting him off. She could feel the heat in her cheeks as that memory resurfaced. As much as Holly wanted to be open and honest with her daughter, there were certain stories she didn't need to here. And that one was most definitely at the top of the list! "If you say one more word, I swear I will stop by your mother's house and spill all the beans you've been hiding from her. And don't you think I won't do it!"

Jake looked horror-stricken at the thought. Gabby, on the other hand, cackled with laughter. Her eyes lit up with amusement, and Holly decided her daughter was enjoying this just a little too much.

Hooking arms with Gabby, Holly smirked at her high school sweetheart. "Well, Jake. It was good to see you again, but Gabby and I must get back to greeting all the guests. You know how it is at these things."

Jake nodded, but the grin he gave her said he saw right through her lame excuse. Not that she really cared. She just wanted to put a bit of distance between Jake and Gabby before he decided to bring up more memories Holly would rather her daughter not hear about.

"So, Jake Holton, huh?" Gabby grinned at her mother. Sometimes Holly thought she might just be a bit too smart for her own good. "I don't think I've ever heard you mention him before. But it looked like you knew him pretty well."

Heat rushed to Holly's cheeks again as she struggled to think of a reply. Anyone with eyes would realize the two of them had a history together, so it shouldn't have been all that surprising Gabby had picked up on it. But how was she supposed to explain him to her? That he was her first love, the man she would have probably still been with if she hadn't moved to Miami and met Gabby's father?

"He's... a friend from high school," Holly said, then winced. It sounded even lamer out loud than it was in her head.

Gabby cackled again. Holly stared into the crowd, avoiding eye contact with her daughter. That just seemed to make Gabby laugh even louder and harder, though. Gabby saw right through her, no doubt, but that didn't mean Holly had to admit anything.

"Oh, look, there's my high school advisor. Let's go say hi," Holly said, abruptly changing directions toward an elderly man leaning against a cane.

Gabby continued to laugh, but she followed her mother through the crowd. As Holly introduced her to various people, Gabby stuck by her side, pleasantly greeting each one of them. Even though Holly hadn't even thought of most of them in decades, they all remembered her clearly and even seemed to have kept up with her life in Miami to an extent.

No doubt that was Nelly's doing. Not only did Nelly have to keep her thumb on Islamorada's pulse, but she had to keep a healthy amount of her own gossip flowing into the grapevine. And it was obvious from the way people talked to her that Nelly had been proud of her eldest daughter.

This, of course, made Holly feel guilty about not having told her mother the truth. She kept telling her it was because Nelly wasn't healthy enough for it yet, wasn't ready to hear the news, but deep down, she knew it was just another lie.

She hadn't told Nelly because she wasn't ready, not her mother. So far, the only ones who knew the truth were her daughter, of course, Jake and Randy, both of whom had kept quiet about the details so far. But Gabby couldn't keep everything a secret for very long.

It had already become public in Miami, and while Miami wasn't exactly right next door to Islamorada, eventually, the news would reach the Keys whether Holly liked it or not. And if Will didn't hurry up and sign the paperwork already, it was liable to become national news once the IRS and SEC got serious.

Holly had the image of herself in handcuffs on the evening news, and she shuddered at the thought. No, that could not happen. She could not let that happen, no matter what. Somehow, she had to make sure Will signed those papers before it was too late.

She could only imagine what was going through her ex-husbands head right then. He already knew he was busted. Unless he pulled off some kind of miracle deal with the IRS, he was almost certainly going to jail. So what did he have to gain from not filling out the paperwork?

Bringing Holly down with him wasn't going to make his situation any easier. If anything, it was just going to make it worse. Gabby and Sean already weren't talking to their father. What would they think of the man if their mother got sent to prison because of him?

A realization hit Holly like a sack of bricks, knocking the air from her lungs. He didn't care, she realized. He didn't care one bit what his kids thought of him. That was why he had been so critical of Holly and her neglect of the kids. It wasn't because he thought she was a bad mother, though he might have. No, it was because he was projecting himself onto her.

She hadn't been mother of the year. But she had never purposely neglected her kids. She had been there for all their important events – sports games, awards ceremonies, etc. If they needed her, Holly had been there for them. She just wasn't a stay at home mother. She was a business woman that had also juggled motherhood and as far as she and her kids were concerned, she did a fine job.

But how many of those games and ceremonies had Will missed? He had always had an excuse for not going. Usually that they couldn't both take time off at the same time, so he would stay at work while Holly attended whatever event was going on.

Now, she knew the truth. He had avoided those events because it would give him the privacy he needed to run the shadier side of his business without Holly looking over his shoulder. He had used their own kids as a smokescreen for his illicit activities.

Holly sighed, and then pushed those thoughts out of her mind. Today was supposed to be a fun day. Not only was it a chance to reconnect with her neighbors, but it was a major step toward bringing the Inn back to life. Holly would eventually figure out what had happened to the funds that should've been in the Inn's accounts, but for now, this would give them the cash they would need to really pay for the renovations and hiring more staff.

All of her other problems could wait until later. For now, she just wanted to live in the moment and enjoy life for a bit.

CHAPTER TWENTY-THREE

Holly slumped against one of the tables. The sun had set a little while ago, and the Archer family was busy cleaning up from the fundraiser. If she had been able to, she would have hired people to manage all of this, but since the whole reason for the fundraiser was how tight on money they were, that left most of the duties to the Archers themselves.

Most of the guests had left already, but a good number were still mingling around, enjoying the gorgeous view of the ocean and the last of the entertainment. Jake was out there somewhere; she was pretty sure. She had lost sight of him while she had been busy cleaning up the food, but she doubted he would leave without saying goodbye.

Her cousins were still around, too, helping with the cleanup. Apparently, they took their role as Archers seriously, and even though the Inn wasn't theirs, they weren't about to leave them in the dust. Holly wasn't sure what she would have done without her cousins. Not just for the fundraiser, but for all the work they had done around the property.

Sure, they were billing the Inn for a lot of work, but Holly had already seen the initial invoices. They weren't charging nearly as much as they'd have charged anyone else. Near as Holly could tell, they were charging just enough to cover the cost of the materials and the wages for their crew, with neither of her cousins taking a cut from the job.

"I can't believe you ever left this place," Gabby said, wandering over to lean against the table with her. She looked just as tired as her mother, her normally pristine hair now frizzy and messy. But she had a smile on her face. A real one, too. "Look how quick everyone in Miami dumped you once they found out about Dad. But here... You've been gone for decades and they all still treat you like you've been here the whole time."

Holly nodded. What Gabby said was true. Even she was in awe at just how many people had come to the fundraiser to help them out. She had expected some of them would want to help, either out of loyalty to the Archer family or just because of the Inn's history. But she really hadn't expected the whole town to stop by at various points.

Music still filled the air and the local D.J. they'd hired was still going strong. Technically, they should have finished up a while ago, since Holly had only paid them for a couple of hours. But even though they were dripping with sweat up on the stage, it was obvious just how much fun they were having. And Holly certainly wasn't going to complain if they wanted to keep the music going for their neighbors.

Holly's phone rang, the sound making both women jump.

They exchanged glances and then laughed. Gabby nudged her mom and winked, then went off to continue with the cleanup while Holly fished out her phone.

"Hello?" she said after accepting the call, not even glancing at the number on the screen.

"Is this Holly Archer?" a deep voice asked from the other end. That voice made her heart skip a beat as she muttered another silent curse. It was her lawyer, and if he was calling her this late at night, she knew it wouldn't be with good news.

"This is her. What's going on, Mr. Marshall?" Holly asked as her mouth went dry. She glanced around for something to drink, but there was nothing nearby. She had already cleaned up most of the stuff where she was, and with the lawyer on the phone, she was hesitant to get any closer to the dwindling crowd.

Thomas Marshall sighed. He was an older man, in his late sixties and the best in the area for this kind of law. She had spared no expense in hiring him, figuring it was worth losing a chunk of her remaining savings if it meant staying out of jail.

"It's Will," he said at last. From the tone of his voice, Holly figured it was more than just him not having signed the papers. And when he continued, he confirmed her worst fears. "He tried to run instead of dealing with the IRS. The FBI picked him up, trying to board a ship to Mexico with a considerable amount of cash on him."

Holly let out the breath she had been holding and gritted her teeth. Her hands balled into fists, and she fought back the urge to start pounding them against the table she still leaned against. He really didn't care about his family, did he? He'd had money stashed away this whole time, and instead of using it to try and make things right, he had tried to leave the country. Leave his family behind to deal with the mess he had created.

"So, what now?" Holly managed to get out. Her entire body was shaking, and she was glad she had stayed a distance away from the rest of the people. She didn't want them to see her like this.

"Well, now it gets tricky," Thomas Marshall said, letting out another tired sigh. "You're going to have to come back to Miami and testify. I've been in contact with both the IRS and the SEC, and I've given them everything I can that proves you had nothing to do with his schemes. They're willing to cut you a deal."

"A deal?" Her mouth went even drier. What kind of deal had they offered? And what would Holly have to give up in exchange for this deal?

"You leaving town right away didn't look good, but when your daughter told me you had gone back to the Keys to help with your family business, I was able to smooth things over. If you come back to Miami and testify under oath about what your ex-husband did, they're willing to drop any pending charges against you. You won't be able to get a realty license again, and I'm sure they'll be watching your finances like hawks for a while, but you also won't be liable for the money Will owes the government."

Holly nodded, though the man couldn't see her. All things considered, it wasn't a bad deal at all. In fact, it was a downright good one. She wouldn't go to prison. She wouldn't be in debt to the IRS for the rest of her life. And, honestly, she had given up any notions of ever going back to real estate.

"As your attorney, I highly suggest you take the deal. The evidence they have is... considerable. The fact that Will tried to leave the country could work in your favor if your charges went to trial, but it's still a crapshoot. But Will is the one they want, not you. And since they legally can't force a wife to testify against her husband, this is their way of putting the final nail in his coffin and giving you what you want at the same time."

"When do I need to be back?"

"As soon as possible. You're scheduled to testify on Wednesday if you accept their deal, but I would prefer it if you came back sooner so we could discuss everything beforehand."

"I'll be there," Holly promised. They only stayed on the line for another moment or two, and then Holly stuffed the phone back into her pocket.

Feeling completely numb, she turned away from the people and the music and the lights and headed down toward the water. It was empty down there on the beach, and while she could still hear the music in the distance, the waves crashing against the shore helped drown them out.

Unable to hold herself together any longer, Holly slumped down onto the sand. Tears fell as she pulled her knees up to her chest, wrapping her arms around them. Squeezing her eyes shut, she let loose, crying without even bothering to fight against it.

The news wasn't bad, not really. It certainly could've been a heck of a lot worse. But it was also the final nail in her coffin as well. Once she went back to Miami, once she stepped foot into that courthouse, her old life really would be over with. There would be no turning back.

And even though she had already known that the phone call with her lawyer had really driven it home. Even if she had wanted to, she had never been able to go back to being the person she had been for the last thirty years. And even though she had been excited to reinvent herself back when she was eighteen, trying to do it again at forty-six was not a fun thought.

She heard the soft footsteps of someone walking along the sand behind her, but she didn't dare open her eyes. She didn't want to know who it was. She just wanted to be left alone for a while—to be able to sit and wallow in her misery.

But of course, that wasn't what the universe had deemed she needed. Someone sat down beside her, but Holly still didn't open her eyes. It wasn't until a strong arm was draped over her shoulder and pulled her against a hard chest that Holly peeked an eye open.

Jake gave her a sad smile and held her tight. He didn't say anything, didn't ask anything. He just sat there and held Holly as the tears continued to stream down her cheeks. Now that they had started, she couldn't make them stop.

If Jake judged her for her breakdown, he didn't show it even a little. He just sat there and held her, even as the noise back up by the Inn started to fade away. Eventually, the music stopped and the sounds of the ocean drowned everything out.

Eventually, her tears subsided and she could breathe again. But when she looked into Jake's eyes, her heart clenched. She couldn't keep lying to him. After everything he had done for her, he deserved the truth.

Before she could stop herself, she told him everything, from start to finish. He sat there quickly, taking it all in. Holly was thankful for his silence. If he had interrupted, even to just ask a question, Holly wasn't sure she would have been able to keep going. But, before she knew it, she had laid it all out for him. All of her secrets were out in the open for him to judge her by.

Except, he didn't. He locked eyes with her for another moment, and then pulled her tight against him again. His chin rested against her forehead. "When do you have to leave?" Jake asked. His voice was low, quiet and soft.

Holly closed her eyes and let out a sigh. Being in his arms, hearing his voice again, it sent her back to high school when he had been the one person she could always count on to comfort her. Even after all those years, she could still count on him, it seemed.

"In a couple of days. I have to testify on Wednesday, but the lawyer wants to talk to me beforehand. So I'll probably have to leave by at least Monday."

Jake nodded. He was quiet for another moment. Then, Holly felt him take a deep breath and let it out slowly. "All right. I'll pack a bag and go with you."

Holly pulled back and stared at him, her mouth gaping open. She blinked a few times; sure that she had misheard him. Comforting her on the beach was one thing, but going back to Miami with her? Not just back to Miami, but going with her to testify against her ex-husband?

Why in the world would he do that?

Jake just gave her a lopsided grin. As if he could read her mind, then he shrugged his shoulders. "I was always there for you, Holly. Why would now be any different?"

"Are... are you sure?" More than anything, Holly wanted him there with her. That thought surprised her a bit, and at the same time, she couldn't just ask him to walk away from his life here for a few days, just to keep her company.

Jake reached out and took her hands in his. He squeezed them and kept his eyes locked on hers, not looking away for even a moment. "I told you back then; you would always be able to trust me—that I would always be there for you. And I meant it, Holly. No matter what."

Holly blinked away the tears that threatened to fall again. She nodded and smiled at him, her heart thundering loud enough to drown out everything. He was one of the very few people she knew she could trust completely.

And she was glad he would be at her side again.

CHAPTER TWENTY-FOUR

Holly tapped her foot against the wooden flooring. Jake sat right next to her, quiet but supportive. Holly had tried to tell him he didn't need to come back up to Miami with her, but nothing she had said could dissuade him.

Gabby had come along, too. Holly hadn't thought that was a good idea either, figuring her daughter didn't need that kind of stress while she was pregnant. But Gabby was just as stubborn, and so the three of them had all driven up together in time for Holly to testify.

Now, they sat side by side in the courtroom on hard wooden benches, waiting. Her lawyers had gone over everything with her, multiple times. All she had to do was tell the truth and she would be golden. That didn't stop her anxiety from going into overdrive, though.

She just wanted to get this all over with. What she would do afterward, she still hadn't figured out. She would return to the Keys most likely. There was still so much work to do around the Inn. Jason and Paul's crew had made good progress already, but it was still going to be another couple of weeks before everything was finished.

Plus, Nelly still wasn't up to running the day to day part of the business yet. Well, she claimed she could handle it just fine, but her doctor disagreed. Cara was there now, helping keep the place afloat while Holly dealt with her own mess.

Jake and Holly had sat by the water for quite a while that night, barely saying a word to each other. And by the time he had escorted her back, the fundraiser had been completely cleaned up, and her family was waiting for her at the house.

One look at their worried faces had been enough to crack the little bit of a shell Holly still had wrapped around herself. So Jake had sat with her again while she told them the story, filling in Gabby on the details she had kept secret. They had all been shocked and outraged at what Will had done, but not one of them had looked at her with pity.

They had all hugged her that night, promising to stand by her, no matter what. Holly couldn't ever remember crying as much as she'd done that night. But she had it all out in the open now, and everyone was ready and willing to help her if she needed them.

She had been more disappointed than she'd expected when Jake had finally left that night. Part of her had wanted to ask him to stay with her, but she bit her tongue. She appreciated everything he had done for her, but she didn't want to rush things.

And now, sitting in the courtroom waiting to testify, she had to fight to keep from reaching out and taking his hand. More than once, she had started to reach out with her hand, but then stopped herself, afraid of what he might think.

Finally, Gabby nudged her. When Holly looked over at her daughter, Gabby gave her a look. She didn't need words for Holly to understand exactly what she meant. Gabby was urging her to go for it, to take that final leap.

She had told Gabby about her relationship with Jake the night before they had driven up to Miami. They had sat in the old Archer family kitchen, shoveling ice cream into their mouths like the sugary treat might make all the pain go away.

Holly took a deep breath, and then went for it. She reached over and put her hand on Jakes. He glanced over at her, smiled, then turned his hand over and threaded his fingers between hers. It may not have been a proclamation of undying love, but it was just what Holly needed to keep her strength up.

And when it was time for her to step onto the stand and look out over the audience, she kept her eyes locked on Jake. He couldn't be up there with her, but he wasn't far away, offering his silent support the entire time.

"And you had no idea your husband was skimming money off the top of each sale?" the prosecutor asked.

Holly shook her head. "He had always wanted us to keep our clients separate from each other. At first, I had just thought it was some kind of little rivalry between us, you know? Who could land the most clients who could sell the biggest house— that kind of thing. It was only after the police showed up that I realize he had kept his clients separate from mine so I wouldn't notice the accounting discrepancies."

The prosecutor nodded, then walked over to his desk and

retrieved a stack of papers. He set them on the stand in front of Holly, and when she leafed through them, she realized they were copies of all the sales she had made in the last ten years or so.

"And these are the sales you'd made yourself, correct?" When Holly nodded, the man took the stack back to his desk. "After a thorough examination of these files, it does appear your accounting was accurate. All money accounted for and all taxes paid."

Holly held her breath. She had known that, of course, but now it was on record. She was almost there, almost in the clear.

"Do you know what your husband was using the money he'd skimmed for?"

Her gaze strayed from Jake to where her ex-husband sat in his orange prison jumpsuit. He glared at her, and she glared right back at him. She had been wondering that same thing until recently. Her lawyer had shown her exactly where the money had gone.

"He was seeing another woman on the side," Holly said, still staring at her ex as she sealed his fate. "Apparently it had been going on for quite some time. He would tell me he had to work late, and then take her out to dinner. Or that he was attending a conference when he was really taking her on a fancy vacation. All the while leaving me to take care of our children. And then he'd tried to use the last of it to flee the country and leave us here to clean up his mess."

She only had to answer a few more questions after that. When she finally stepped down from the stand and headed for the door, her shoulders were lighter. The burden Will had dumped onto her was gone now. He would no doubt rot in prison for quite some time, but Holly would never again have to worry about going down because of him.

Holly had barely passed through the little swinging gate that separated the observers from the rest of the courtroom when Jake rushed over and wrapped her in a tight bear hug. Holly leaned against him, smiling, and not caring who saw the two of them together.

Her marriage was over. Her business was over. And now, the life she'd had in Miami was finally over. Now, she could focus on the next phase of her life – rebuilding the family Inn and dedicating a lot more time to her mother, kids and grandkids.

Gabby hugged her next, squeezing her almost as tight as Jake had. When they pulled apart, Gabby smiled at her for a moment. Then, she looked over in the direction of her father and shot him an icy glare. Holly didn't bother looking to see if Will was watching them. She knew he was.

Instead, she took her daughter's hand and Jake's, and then they all headed out of the courtroom together.

One problem down, only a million more to go. But despite the daunting list of tasks ahead of her, Holly had a renewed sense of energy. She could do this, and she felt it in every bone in her body. No matter what curveballs life threw at her, she could do this.

And she wasn't alone. She would never have to worry about being alone ever again.

CHAPTER TWENTY-FIVE

"I THINK WE NEED TO CELEBRATE," GABBY DECLARED AS THE three of them left the courthouse. She grinned broadly as if nothing in the world could possibly go wrong. Her excitement was contagious and Holly and Jake grinned as well.

"What did you have in mind?" Holly asked, raising an eyebrow. With Gabby, she didn't always know what to expect. It could've been anything from a simple family dinner to a full-blown party if she wasn't careful.

"Dinner at that little Italian place, you used to take us as a treat when we were kids."

Holly raised an eyebrow. That place hadn't been anything special, just a little mom and pop restaurant that hadn't been too far from their house. But whenever the kids had done something worth celebrating, that was where they had always wanted to go.

It wouldn't have been Holly's first choice, but if that was what Gabby wanted, who was she to argue?

"We'll have to call Sean and let him know how it went. And invite him along," Holly said as they headed toward the cars.

She would fill him in on everything as well. He had wanted to be there with her in court, but Shawna hadn't been able to get off work, so Sean had been watching their daughter. That was one thing Holly had put her foot down over. She wasn't going to let her granddaughter witness any of their turmoil. She was only three, and she didn't need this kind of stress in her young life, and Sean had agreed.

Gabby smirked at the mention of her brother, and then made a sour face. "Do we have to? Can't we just invite Shawna and Rachel and leave him home?"

Holly playfully smacked her daughter's shoulder. She doubted they would ever truly stop their sibling bickering, and she honestly hoped they never did. She didn't want her kids to grow apart like she had done with her own siblings.

She had managed to rekindle things with her brother, but she still had a long way to go with her sisters. She hadn't spoken to Rina since that night, and though Randy had filled Amy in on everything going on with the Inn and their mother, Holly still hadn't gotten up the courage to call her.

When they finally reached Gabby's house, they found her fiancé looking like he had been through the wringer a few times. The moment he locked eyes on Gabby, he rushed over to hug her, making her squeak at the suddenness.

"Oh, thank, God!" he practically yelled. He blinked a few times like he was on the verge of tears. "When you ran off to the Keys to track down your mother and then called to say you were staying there for a while, I thought..."

"You thought I wasn't coming back," Gabby finished for him, and he nodded.

Gabby sighed as she hugged her fiancé back. Holly knew Gabby had been considering doing just that, at least for a little while. But Holly also knew Gabby had sorted through most of the insecurities they'd been having and was ready to face whatever life threw at her.

"Come on, let's go sit down." Gabby took Lucas's hand and guided him toward their living room. Holly and Jake headed for the kitchen to give the two of them some privacy, but their apartment wasn't very big and they could hear everything that was said.

"I'm so sorry I scared you like that. I was just... I was going through some stuff, and I needed to talk to Mom first. I now know I should have talked to you first instead."

"What's going on, baby? Did I do something to upset you?"

"No, it wasn't anything you did." Gabby took a deep breath. "It was just... all this stuff with my father; it kinda hit me all at once. It freaked me out, and I started having some crazy and irrational thoughts. But Mom helped talk some sense into me, though."

There was silence for a few moments. Holly could only imagine what went through their minds right then. She knew Gabby had to be on pins and needles, getting ready to give her future husband the big news.

"Lucas, there's something else. I'm.... I'm pregnant. We're going to have a baby."

The silence that followed only lasted for a brief second. Then, Lucas's shouting filled the apartment. "What? Oh my, God! Really? Are you sure? Have you been to the doctor yet?" He asked a dozen questions, one after another, not even giving Gabby a chance to breathe, let alone answer.

Holly and Jake exchanged smiles as they listened to them celebrate their upcoming child. Will had certainly never reacted like that when she had given him the news about their children and that alone told Holly her daughter would be just fine.

Lucas wasn't Will. He wouldn't do the same things Will had done. He wouldn't put his family at risk, wouldn't jeopardize their futures and happiness, just to satisfy his own needs and desires. All of the fears Gabby had about her relationship, turning out just like her mothers, were completely unfounded.

"Think it's safe to go in there?" Jake whispered. His eyes darted in the direction of the living room. "Or do you think they're going to try and rope us into baby shower planning or something?"

Holly laughed, then took his hand and led him to the living room. After introducing Jake to Lucas, it was indeed baby-mania for a little while. Eventually, Holly slipped off and called Sean, giving him an update on how court had gone and invited them to the little celebration dinner.

Except, now it wasn't just a dinner for Holly. It was one for Gabby, too. Now that she had told Lucas about the baby, there was no point in keeping it a secret anymore.

Holly had planned on driving back down to the Keys that night, but by the time they finished their celebration dinner, it was far too late to travel. Gabby, of course, insisted they stay at the apartment for the night and wouldn't take no for an answer.

For a brief moment, Holly had a vision of her and Jake curled up together in the guest room, sleeping in each other's arms for the night. But Jake, ever the gentleman, had taken the couch instead, leaving Holly's dream just that.

CHAPTER TWENTY-SIX

"Thanks for going with me," Holly told Jake as they walked hand-in-hand along the beach. The sun was quickly setting, coating everything in yellows and oranges and reds.

They had spent most of the day in Miami with Holly's family. She had wanted to get back on the road right away, knowing Cara was already doing her a huge favor by managing everything while she was gone. But since she had already neglected her family enough in the pursuit of one job, she wasn't about to do it again and had agreed to stick around for a bit.

Which meant it was almost nightfall by the time they had gotten back to the Inn.

The Inn hadn't burned to the ground in her absence, and between the time she had spent with her kids and the long drive back down to the islands, Holly had had a lot of time to think. And, for the first time in about a year, she wasn't afraid to be left alone with her thoughts for an extended period of time.

"Anytime. Just try not to get on the IRS's bad side again," Jake teased, flashing her a wide grin.

Holly rolled her eyes. As if Jake had needed more ammunition to tease her about. It was bad enough he knew all of her childhood secrets. But he was just so easy to talk to and be around, and there was no one she trusted quite like him.

"I was thinking," Holly said, changing the subject abruptly. "I've spent too much time neglecting my family. I was in such a rush to get away from here, and I had left everyone I cared about behind. I think I'm going to reach out to Rina and Amy, see if I can get them back to the house for at least a little while. Mom's got her seventieth birthday coming up soon, and I figure that's the perfect chance to get everyone together again."

Jake nodded. He squeezed her hand, and then turned to pull her into his arms. "I think that's a wonderful idea. What does that mean for us, then?"

"What do you want it to mean?" Holly chewed on her bottom lip as she looked up at him. She'd been having these thoughts about Jake since she'd first laid eyes on him at Melissa's party. Now, it was time to find out if he felt the same way or if she was the only one getting lost in nostalgic memories.

"I think you know what I want, Holly. I want you. I've missed you more than I ever thought I would. I always figured we were young, that I would find someone else to share my life with. But after all those years, I never did. Not until you walked back into my life."

Holly's throat tightened as she nodded. Those were the words she had wanted to hear, but that didn't stop her heart from racing faster and faster with each passing moment. "Then I think we should give it a shot again. See where life takes us."

"I like the sound of that."

Jake moved as if in slow motion. Holly watched wide-eyed as his face inched closer and closer to hers. When their lips finally touched, it sent off a cascade of explosions throughout her body as they kissed. She leaned against him, closing her eyes and letting the warmth from the setting sun wash over them.

Maybe forty-six really wasn't too late to start over again...

You can now Pre – Order
Book Two – Secrets in Paradise

Only for Subscribers
The Archer House Epilogue

Other Books by Kimberly

The Archer Inn Series

Secrets in Paradise
When The Stars Align

9 781393 251866